A DATE WITH ROMANCE

Refusing to live in the shadow of her father, a famous TV chef, Lauren Tate runs her own cake shop with her best friend, Daisy. Having been unlucky in love, Lauren pours her energy into her business — until she meets her handsome new neighbour, Jake, who is keen to strike up a friendship with her. Will Lauren decide to take him up on the offer? Then Daisy has an accident, and announces she'll be following her partner to America once she has healed — leaving Lauren with some difficult choices . . .

TONI ANDERS

◆

A DATE
WITH
ROMANCE

Complete and Unabridged

LINFORD
Leicester

First published in Great Britain in 2016

First Linford Edition
published 2017

A catalogue record for this book is available
from the British Library.

ISBN 978–1–4448–3218–1

Published by
F. A. Thorpe (Publishing)
Anstey, Leicestershire

Set by Words & Graphics Ltd.
Anstey, Leicestershire
Printed and bound in Great Britain by
T. J. International Ltd., Padstow, Cornwall

This book is printed on acid-free paper

1

'Oh no! What on earth!' Lauren picked her way over a mound of goatskin rugs, violently patterned cushions, cardboard boxes, books tied in bundles and a battered guitar littering the corridor outside her flat.

'Ouch!' She caught her ankle against a small upended coffee table. The door of the flat opposite was open, revealing cardboard boxes and piles of books and clothes. There was no sign of its occupant.

A plastic bag sagged against her front door. She kicked it aside and a pile of large muddy trainers fell out. Muttering to herself, she opened the door of her flat and slipped hurriedly inside. She had no desire to meet her new untidy neighbour.

The neatness of her own flat soothed her. The bowl of white daisies on the windowsill shone in the late afternoon sunshine, and there was a faint scent of lavender from the polish she had used the evening before.

She went into the bright little red and white kitchen and made herself a cup of coffee. Then she switched on just one bar of her electric fire, lay back in an armchair, and closed her eyes.

Did she really want to go to Daisy's jewellery party this evening? The answer was no, but she'd promised Daisy and didn't want to let her down. She knew she'd enjoy it once she was there, but after a tiring day at work it was an effort to get ready for an evening out. She sighed. Perhaps when she'd finished her coffee and had a shower with her new magnolia shower cream, she'd feel more like going out.

She stretched her legs and thought of the muddle in the corridor. So flat number twelve was taken again. A picture of its last owner came into her mind. Steve. Steve of the laughing suntanned face and copper-coloured hair. Steve who'd almost become her fiancé. He'd been gone six weeks, and at last she could think of him

2

without her eyes filling with tears.

This time she wouldn't get involved with the occupant of flat number twelve, however attractive he might be. This time she'd keep herself to herself. Of course it could be a woman, but somehow she didn't think so. Those grubby trainers had been very large.

She took her coffee cup into the kitchen, rinsed it and went into the bedroom. The wardrobe door creaked as she opened it and gazed without enthusiasm at the contents. Perhaps she should buy some new clothes. She was tired of wearing the same old things. But since Steve had left … Well never mind that, what should she wear tonight?

She pushed trousers to one side. A jewellery party deserved a dress. She reached for an old faithful — mustard jersey with cap sleeves and a twirly skirt. It always looked good with her heavy gold necklace. She pulled out her black patent shoes with high heels — not very comfortable, but she'd be mostly sitting down — and closed the wardrobe door.

As she did so, there was a ring at the doorbell.

'Good thing I hadn't started to undress,' she muttered. It was probably Graham, the janitor, about the broken window at the end of the corridor. About time. She'd mentioned it on a dozen occasions. She flung open the door.

'Well! Worth waiting for!'

A young man lounged against the door jamb. Young man? That was an inadequate description. Perhaps stand-in for a Greek god would be more accurate.

Lauren gaped, a slow blush flooding her cheeks. The Greek god smiled at her. Thick, black curly hair flopped over his forehead. His eyes were a deep sapphire blue like the waters of the Aegean Sea. Lauren had never seen the Aegean Sea but was sure the blue was the blue of his eyes.

He put a finger under her chin and closed her mouth. 'That's better.'

Feeling foolish, she stepped back into her flat. No involvement, no matter how attractive, she reminded herself.

4

A hand was thrust towards her. 'Jake Viner. I'm your new neighbour.' He flashed a wide smile.

Reluctantly she gave him her hand. 'Lauren Tate.'

'May I come in? I'd like to get acquainted.'

She looked past him at the pile of assorted objects on the landing. They were still there. He turned and followed her gaze.

'Oh yes. I'm sorry. I'm not very good at tidying up. But I'll do it soon. That's why I called in. I can't find my coffee. I know I bought some, but it's disappeared.' He ran his fingers through his curls. 'I wondered whether you could lend me some.'

'It's usually sugar,' she said automatically.

'I beg your pardon?'

'Neighbours usually borrow sugar.'

'Don't take it,' he said.

Don't say I'm sweet enough, she begged silently. He didn't.

'If you don't want to lend it, perhaps you'd make me a cup of coffee. I need coffee every hour to keep me going,' he said seriously. 'I'll have that mess in the corridor cleared up in no time if I have a cup of coffee.'

What a cheek, she thought. A complete stranger!

'I'm going out,' she said coldly. 'I haven't time to make coffee or chat. I'll get you a jar. I have a spare one.'

He stepped into her flat and started to close the door.

'No. Leave it open, please.' *I'm not that trusting*, she thought. *I don't know you.* She took a jar of coffee from the cupboard and heard him jingle the coins in his pocket. 'Keep it,' she said, stopping his thanks. 'It's a housewarming present.'

* ★ ★ ★ *

She arrived late at Daisy's party. Her friends were all there, excitedly examining gold and silver chains, holding up the objects they most desired. Necklaces and bracelets of pink, green, blue and gold were piled invitingly on the table.

6

Sparkling earrings lay temptingly on blue velvet pads. The saleswoman had provided several mirrors on stands, and these were placed around the table.

Jane waved an arm as Lauren entered the room, her arm decorated with six bracelets. 'I can't decide which I like best,' she sighed.

'Hi, Lauren,' Claire called. 'What about this?' She settled a small tiara decorated with blue and white stones on her black curls.

'Lovely,' Lauren called back. 'Are you getting married again?'

'What happened to you?' asked Daisy. 'I thought you were coming early so that we could have first look.'

'New neighbour. He's taken the flat opposite.'

'The one where Steve —'

'He came over to introduce himself and borrow some coffee.'

'Should be sugar,' said Daisy automatically.

Lauren glared at her. 'He had the cheek to ask me to make him a cup of coffee.'

Lauren removed her coat and threw it on to Daisy's bed.

'What's he like?' Daisy was curious. 'Young, old, tall, short? Not another Australian?'

'English. Tall, dark and —'

'Handsome,' Daisy finished for her.

Lauren felt herself blushing and turned away. 'It doesn't matter. I'm not interested.'

'I'm worried about you.' Daisy poured her a glass of white wine. 'You haven't been out with anyone since Steve left. That's five or six weeks ago.'

'So?'

'You need a boyfriend. You belong in a pair.'

'What a crazy idea. You mean I can't function without a man?'

'I don't mean that.' Daisy's brown face looked apologetic. 'You're the most capable woman I know. But you like to go out, to have fun. It's better with a partner.'

Lauren knew Daisy was thinking of her own partner, Morice; a large, lovable jazz musician who adored Daisy. She picked up her wine glass and stood up. 'Come on. Let's look at the bling. I'm in a spending mood.'

'Good.' Daisy followed her into the sitting-room and claimed a mirror for them both.

For the next hour Lauren forgot Jake, Steve and all other men while she tried on necklaces, earrings, bracelets and hair ornaments.

'Are you buying all those?' asked Claire, looking at the pile in front of Lauren. 'Leave some for us.'

Lauren laughed. 'I just might have all these.'

When it came to reckoning time, Lauren decided she would spend only thirty pounds, but was satisfied with her rose quartz necklace and bracelet of tiny blue flowers.

Everyone helped the saleswoman to pack away her wares while Daisy and Lauren made coffee and opened a bottle of wine. There was a lot of laughing and joking; the girls were pleased with their purchases and Lauren, placing plates of cakes and nibbles on the table, smiled happily at her friends and joined in the banter. What did Daisy mean? She didn't need a man when she had friends like these.

But was she right. Daisy had Morice, Claire and Jane had husbands, and Lisa was engaged. Everyone had someone to go home to, or at least relate to. Only she was completely on her own. She felt a little shiver down her spine. Time to change the subject. She picked up the coffee pot. 'Refills, anyone?'

When the others had gone, Daisy and Lauren curled up in armchairs and Daisy returned to the subject. 'Tell me more about your mysterious new neighbour.'

'I know nothing about him.' Lauren stretched over to take a tiny sausage roll. 'He's tall, dark and —'

'Handsome,' supplied Daisy again.

'All right, handsome,' agreed Lauren. 'We only spoke for a few minutes. I can't tell you anything else. Except his name. Jake Viner.'

'Mm.' Daisy looked thoughtful. 'Jake

10

Viner. You've heard nothing of Steve since he left?' She tried to sound casual, knowing that Lauren could flare up at the mention of his name.

Lauren looked down into her cup. 'We agreed not to write. He's probably engaged by now. I'm sure he had someone back home. She sighed. 'I was fool enough to hope he'd find me more attractive and stay here.'

'He said he was in England for only a year,' Daisy gently reminded her.

Lauren shifted her position in her chair. 'I know. I keep telling myself that. Anyway, it's all over now. Let's not talk about it.'

Daisy poured them both some more coffee. 'Did you think any more about the chocolate and mint cupcakes?'

'I tried them at the weekend. Not very successful. You try. I'm going to concentrate on coffee flavours for a bit.'

They were soon deep in conversation about cakes. Then Daisy put down her cup. 'I've got a surprise for you.' She darted into the kitchen and came back with a plastic box. She opened it with a flourish and displayed the contents to her friend.

'Daisy! What's this?' Lauren reached into the box and brought out a cupcake. It was pale green and a small chocolate flake lay across the top.

'Try it,' Daisy urged. 'Honest opinion.'

Lauren ate slowly and thoughtfully, then her face broke into a smile. 'Perfect. Can't fail.' She took another bite. 'When did you make these?'

'Last night. If you'd done well with the mint and chocolate, I'd have kept quiet but as you don't seem keen on making them ...'

'Perfect,' said Lauren again. 'I'm glad mine were no good. We'll make some tomorrow and try them in the shop, shall we?'

'I've got five dozen ready for decorating,' said Daisy. 'We can go in early tomorrow and have them ready in no time.'

There was the rattle of a key in the front door. Daisy glanced at the clock.

'That's Morice. He said he'd call in.'

As she spoke, a large young man with a shiny black face and long corkscrew curls exploded into the room. 'Where's my little Daisy-belle?' He grabbed Daisy in a bear hug and danced her round the room. Spotting Lauren in a chair, he swooped on her and she received a bear hug too.

'Oh Morice, don't be so rough,' she protested, laughing.

The man standing just inside the door and watching the scene seemed as quiet as Morice was exuberant. Morice dragged him forward.

'This is Ray. He's new to the band. New to the area. I'm going to introduce him to a few people. First, this is my beautiful Daisy.'

Ray and Daisy smiled at each other. 'Coffee?' asked Daisy, and she went into the kitchen.

'And this is our friend, Lauren.'

Ray shook Lauren's hand. 'Also beautiful.'

'Lauren's heart-free at the moment,'

went on the irrepressible Morice. 'Play your cards right and you never know your luck.'

Lauren looked at Ray and was glad to see he looked as embarrassed as she felt.

Before anyone could speak, Morice spotted the cakes. 'Oh boy!' he said, and helped himself. He passed the box to Ray. 'Dig in. They'll have plenty more. They make them.'

Ray looked at Lauren and raised his eyebrows.

Daisy came back into the room in time to rescue the last two cakes. 'These are prototypes.' She fastened the lid firmly on to the box. 'Don't you dare eat the last two.'

She produced a plate of sandwiches and the men began to tuck in. Ray proved to be not as shy as he'd seemed at first, and the group were soon laughing and joking.

'I've got an idea,' said Morice to Daisy. 'Why don't you and Lauren come along to the club on Saturday? We've got some guest artistes, so we shan't be playing all evening. We can dance. That'll be fun.'

Lauren looked at Ray's solemn face and spiky fair hair. He wasn't her idea of a boyfriend, but he was friendly and pleasant. The evening might be fun. She grinned at Daisy. 'I'm game if you are.'

* * *

On the way home, Lauren wondered why she'd agreed to Morice's suggestion. Ray might think she saw him as a possible boyfriend. What if they didn't get on? She would be stuck with him for a whole evening. But what was one evening? There needn't be a repeat.

Daisy wasn't the only one of their crowd determined to find her a replacement for Steve. Despite her protests, each friend saw it as her duty to provide Lauren with another partner.

Lauren smiled to herself. Perhaps she should go along with the idea. Perhaps she did need a special someone. Anyway, she'd have some interesting times finding out. But not Jake. Not another man living so near that he'd get under her skin, and when he left he'd leave a hole in her heart. She'd go along with her friends' ideas, however crazy, and then maybe they'd leave her alone to concentrate on her future business plans.

She parked the car and made her way upstairs to her flat. She put the key into the lock but before she could turn it, the door of the flat opposite flew open.

'I've been waiting for you,' said Jake. 'Have you had a good evening?'

Lauren looked at him in surprise. 'Very good, thank you.' She pushed open the door.

'No.' Jake came across the corridor. 'Don't go in yet. I want to show you my tidy flat. I told you that a cup of coffee would spur me on. Come and see the result.'

Reluctantly, Lauren closed her door again. It was difficult to resist the eager, puppy-like grin on Jake's face.

'I want someone to appreciate my hard work.' He shepherded her across the corridor and into his flat. 'I know, leave the door open,' he said before she could speak.

Lauren felt very strange being in the flat she had known so well. But of course it had looked very different in Steve's time. The basic furniture was the same — the flats were let furnished; but whereas Steve had shown little interest in rugs and cushions, preferring a minimalist home, Jake obviously liked his comfort. Cushions in a rainbow of colours covered the couch and chairs: big, fat, squashy cushions inviting you to sink into them. There were bright prints on the walls, and even ornaments on the windowsill. The effect was warm and inviting.

He flung open the bedroom door. 'I've done this room too.'

Lauren peeped over his shoulder but refused to go in. She took in a plum and cream duvet with matching curtains and a white Flokati rug on the floor. A bookcase in the living room was crowded with a variety of books and CDs. Lauren was amused to see that all the bundles and boxes had disappeared — presumably he'd found a place for everything.

'You're impressed, I can see,' Jake said with a grin.

'You've done very well,' she admitted. 'It looks very nice. Warm and comfy.'

'Can I offer you a drink? Some of your own coffee, or some wine?'

Don't get involved, Lauren reminded herself. *It'll be Steve all over again.* 'No thank you.' She walked towards the door. 'It's late. I have work tomorrow, and I expect you have too.'

'Oh well, another time.' He didn't attempt to persuade her. 'I'll walk you home.'

Lauren tightened her lips to hide a smile as he put a hand under her elbow and conducted her the two or three steps across the corridor to her own door, which she then unlocked. 'Good night,' she said.

He put a hand on her arm. 'Lauren, we can be friends, can't we?'

'Of course.' Whatever that meant, she thought. Perhaps it just meant lending him some coffee.

'Good night,' she said again, and went

quickly into her flat before he could continue the conversation. Inside she went straight to her bedroom to prepare for bed. She was tired. It had been an eventful evening.

She was about to get into bed when the telephone rang. 'Did you catch the show, Pidge?'

'Dad! No, I'm sorry. I was at Daisy's. I've just come in.'

'Never mind. I recorded it. Went very well. My new assistant will be a sensation.'

'Oh Dad, not another fluffy blonde who's using you as a stepping stone to becoming a TV presenter!'

'This one really wants to cook. And she's nice. Wait till you meet her. When are you coming for a meal? We haven't seen you here for ages.'

'Two weeks, to be exact.'

'Well, it seems ages.'

'I'll come soon. Promise. I'll surprise you.'

'Right. See you then. Night, Pidge.'

'Goodnight, Dad.' Lauren replaced the phone and switched off the light. For a while she stared into the darkness, thinking first of Steve then of Jake. Gently, she drifted into sleep.

2

Lauren and Daisy were hard at work by seven o'clock the next morning, topping the new cupcakes with pretty mint-green cream and gently adding a small chocolate flake to each one. Lauren arranged them on large trays and took them into the shop.

'I think I'll make some of my coffee cakes now,' she told Daisy, 'and perhaps a few strawberry ones. They're very popular.' She assembled flour, sugar and eggs while Daisy scrubbed the table they'd used for the mint and chocolate cupcakes.

'We'll have a coffee now,' Daisy decided, 'before the rush begins.'

'My father phoned last night,' said Lauren. 'He has a new assistant. He says she's keen on cooking.'

'That'll make a change,' said Daisy. 'They're usually fluffy dolly birds. Where on earth does he find them?'

'No idea,' said Lauren, slipping the tray of cakes into the oven. 'But his antics make life interesting. I shouldn't like an ordinary, boring father.'

'It must be nice having a famous TV chef as your dad.' Daisy poured two cups of coffee. 'Why aren't you his assistant?'

'I should hate to be on television and have everyone looking at me and criticising my appearance.' Lauren took her place at the table and picked up her coffee cup.

Daisy looked at her friend. Lauren's dark auburn hair and bright hazel eyes would contrast well on TV with the blondes her father favoured. But Lauren wasn't the slightest bit vain and wouldn't push herself forward.

'He suggested it once,' Lauren went on, 'but I made it plain I wanted my own career, not to ride on his coat-tails.'

'That's why you have your own cake business?'

'Certainly. I don't want comparisons with him. I want to make a success of a different aspect of cooking.'

'Good for you. I'm sure you'll do it. With my help, of course.' They smiled at each other.

'Changing the subject, what did you think of Morice's friend last night?'

Lauren gave her a sideways glance. 'You don't give up, do you? He's very pleasant, but I don't want a boyfriend.'

'But you're coming to the club? You're not trying to get out of it?'

'Of course not. I'm looking forward to it. I'm just making the situation plain, that's all. And you can tell Morice too. I could see hearts and flowers floating in front of his eyes.'

'Morice is a romantic,' said Daisy. 'He'd like you to be as happy as we are.'

'He's a sweetie,' said Lauren. 'You're very lucky.' She opened the oven door and slid out the tray of cakes. The kitchen was filled with the warm aroma of baking. Lauren sniffed. 'I love this smell.' She put the tray on the table and placed another in the oven. 'What are you wearing on Saturday?' she asked, folding some aprons and placing them on a shelf.

'I've got a new blue and purple maxi dress,' said Daisy. 'What about you?'

'Goodness knows. I was thinking last night that I need some new clothes.'

'Let's go shopping on Wednesday afternoon when the shop's closed,' suggested Daisy. 'I could do with some new shoes. We could have tea at that posh café in Bridge Street. See if their cakes match up to ours.'

'Look at the clock!' Lauren hastily swallowed the last drop of coffee and jumped out of her seat. 'Eight thirty! Nearly time to open up.'

There was no time for talking as they hurried to arrange the trays and plates of cakes ready for the morning rush.

Lauren's old school friend, Jane, rang at lunchtime. 'You're still coming tomorrow, aren't you?'

'Coming? Um … where?' Lauren asked cautiously.

'Oh Lauren. You are hopeless. We talked about it last week. To the operatic society.'

Operatic society, thought Lauren in

24

horror. Surely she couldn't have agreed to go there.

'You promised,' Jane reminded her.

I must have been mad, thought Lauren, unable to think of a reply.

'We were at that karaoke club,' said Jane, 'and you said how much you loved singing. So I suggested you come along to the society.'

'Well if I promised …' Lauren said doubtfully.

'You did. You promised to come with me tomorrow.'

'Very well. Pick me up. What time?'

Arrangements were made and Lauren replaced the telephone. She made a face at Daisy. 'Apparently I promised to go with Jane to her operatic society tomorrow. I don't remember promising.'

'Jane's very keen,' said Daisy. 'You'll be tied down to one evening a week for months.'

'I won't.' Lauren changed into a clean apron and threw another at Daisy. 'I agreed to go tomorrow. I didn't say anything about after that.'

Daisy's mint and chocolate cupcakes were a great success. She gave Lauren a triumphant grin as she sold the last two.

'Told you they were perfect,' said Lauren. 'They'll be a regular line now.'

* * *

The next afternoon was early closing. Lauren and Daisy set off for town as soon as they'd cleaned up and left the shop ready for the morning.

'I think I'll get a maxi dress too,' said Lauren. 'It'll be useful for holidays. Where shall I look first?'

They tried a large department store, searching through rails of dresses long and short.

'I can't see anything that I like,' moaned Lauren. 'Where did you buy your dress?'

'A little shop in that alley near the church. I'll take you.'

The shop was attractive, the owner helpful, but still Lauren couldn't find anything that she liked.

'There's a new boutique in Market

Street,' she suggested doubtfully. 'It was advertising in the local rag. We could try there.'

They found the shop without much difficulty and went in. 'This is more like it,' said Lauren, smiling. The dresses were well displayed on hangers suspended from hooks around the walls. 'Look at that one,' she breathed. 'D'you think it'll be expensive?'

She moved towards a cream and soft green striped dress, gathered under the bust and with elbow-length sleeves. An assistant popped out from somewhere and offered to show her the fitting room. Ten minutes later Daisy was nodding in approval as Lauren pirouetted in front of her.

The price had caused Lauren a moment's hesitation, but another glance in a full-length mirror did it for her. *I'll have it*, she decided, *and blow the cost*.

Before they left the shop, Lauren had tried on and purchased two more dresses, and Daisy had fallen for an embroidered evening jacket.

'We'd better have our tea and recover,' said Daisy with a laugh as they left the shop. 'I had no intention of buying anything this afternoon except some shoes. Why did I buy a jacket?'

Lauren joined in the laughter. 'For the same reason that I went in to buy one dress and came out with three. Because they were beautiful.'

In the café they examined the cakes critically.

'We've had no lunch,' said Daisy, 'so we can have two different ones each.'

'And give them marks out of ten,' suggested Lauren. She chose a coffee cream slice and a strawberry meringue. Daisy settled for a peach shortcake and a pineapple cream.

They ate in silence. When the cakes were finished, Lauren turned a solemn face to Daisy. 'I'm afraid they're delicious.'

Daisy nodded. 'I have to admit they're almost as good as our own. What marks shall we give them?'

'It has to be a ten,' said Lauren mournfully. Their giggles turned to laughter which they had difficulty stifling.

'It doesn't matter,' said Daisy at last. 'They have a café, we have a shop. We're not rivals. Have another cup of tea. I've still got some shoes to get, then we can go home.'

★　★　★

The operatic society held their rehearsals in a gloomy old school building. Lauren looked around her without enthusiasm. What a place to spend an evening.

Jane caught her expression. 'Cheer up. We're not here for the décor. Come along, I'll introduce you to the director.'

The director, Gordon, was a short, plump man with a worried expression. Jane introduced Lauren and he brightened up.

'We don't get many pretty young ladies wanting to join,' he said. 'The women we get finished going to clubs years ago, if they ever went. Of course they can all sing,' he went on gloomily. 'Never mind. Can you dance, Miss — er — um …'

'I'm Lauren. What sort of dancing?'

'Any sort. Ballet, tap, ballroom ...'

'Well,' Lauren began, before being interrupted by a lissom young blonde in a leotard.

'Chloe, our choreographer,' said Gordon.

Chloe barely nodded at Lauren. 'Can we start with the ballroom scene? I have some new moves to try out.' Without waiting for Gordon's consent, Chloe dashed off.

'Thinks a lot of herself,' Jane muttered. 'She's good but she knows it.'

'I thought this was an operatic society, not a dance company,' said Lauren. 'What about the singing?'

'The chorus are singing at the sides in this scene,' explained Jane. 'The dancers will be in the middle.'

'Are you a dancer?'

'Me?' Jane gave a short laugh. 'I don't think I'm built for dancing. No, I'm in the chorus.'

Gordon came hurrying up. 'Young lady. Lauren, is it? Come with me.' He led

Lauren to the centre of the room where five couples and a lone young man stood waiting for instructions.

'Alan knows what to do. He'll lead you,' said Gordon, hurrying off. Lauren was left facing the young man.

'I've had a different partner for the last three weeks,' grumbled Alan. 'I hope you can waltz.'

'I think I can manage that,' Lauren said coldly.

Surprisingly, he gave her a smile. 'I'm sorry. It's not your fault, but every week my partner disappears and Gordon produces someone else.' He held out a hand. 'I'm Alan.'

She shook his hand. 'Lauren. It's my first time here. You'll have to push me around.'

Before they could say any more, the bossy choreographer appeared. 'Places everyone,' she called. 'Are we ready? And one, two, three.' The music started, Alan took Lauren in his arms, and they danced round the stage, into the middle and out, the women making a star in the centre

31

and out again to their partners.

Later, Lauren couldn't imagine how she'd got through the routine. Alan was an excellent partner, but it took all her concentration to follow him and not make a complete mess of the dance. She dared not look at the choreographer watching them intently from the front of the group, and gave a sigh of relief when the woman ignored her and went to speak to a couple at the back.

'Jolly good,' said Alan. 'You did very well.'

She gave him a smile of thanks and escaped to find Jane. Jane was waiting for her with two cups of coffee.

'I thought I came to sing,' Lauren complained.

'I'm sorry,' said Jane. 'Gordon grabs anyone who might make a dancer. They're few and far between. When the break is over we'll all be singing. There are some lovely songs in this show.'

They sipped their coffee, then Jane gave a bright smile. 'What do you think of Alan? Quite a few of the girls fancy him.'

Lauren gave her a cold look. 'Did you get me here for some reason other than singing?'

'Of course not,' Jane blustered. 'It's just that I happen to know that he finished with his girlfriend two weeks ago, and —'

'And I might fill the vacant place. Please, Jane, don't bother.'

Lauren surveyed the noisy crowd around her. There were far more women than men, and most of them were much older than her. Did she really want to spend her precious evenings here? She didn't think so.

Alan came over and took the vacant seat next to her. 'You did very well if you're not a dancer,' he said. 'Are you going to join us?'

Before Lauren could answer, Jane said, 'I'll just go and see Gordon about your audition when we finish.'

'Audition?' Lauren was startled.

'Just a formality,' said Alan. 'You'll be accepted.'

Lauren looked thoughtful. *I must get out of this before it goes any further,* she decided. Then she realised Alan was speaking to her.

'Would you mind being my partner in the ballroom scene? We'll do well together.'

Lauren looked at his serious face, slightly shiny from his exertions. It was a nice face, not handsome but friendly. She was sure that Jane would consider him just right for her. She stood up. 'I must go. Would you tell Jane I'll ring her tomorrow evening?'

When she got outside she remembered that she'd come in Jane's car. The rain, which had earlier been a light drizzle, began to come down in earnest. Darting back into the shelter of the doorway, she fumbled for her mobile phone and ordered a taxi, keeping an eye open for an irate Jane.

The taxi arrived and in ten minutes Lauren was back in her block of flats. When she reached her flat she realised that the door of number twelve was slightly ajar. She was wondering whether she could open her door quietly enough not to attract Jake's attention when he appeared carrying a parcel.

'I took this in for you,' he explained. 'Saves you going to the sorting office to collect it.'

'That's very kind of you.' She took the parcel. 'Would you ...' She looked at him. 'Would you like to come in for a nightcap?'

'I should like that very much.' He darted across and closed his door and in a second was following her into her flat. She turned to find him holding open the door, a quizzical expression on his face.

'Please close it,' she said, and went into the kitchen. She came back with a bottle and two glasses. 'I'm afraid I've only got white wine.'

'Suits me,' he said. 'I thought you might mean coffee, and you know what that does to me. I'd be up all night doing housework.'

Lauren poured the wine and handed him a glass. 'We can't have that. You'd keep us all awake.'

As he sipped his wine, Lauren took a

quick glance at him. His hair was tidier than when she'd first seen him. His jeans and shirt were much cleaner. Obviously he wanted to make a good impression.

'Have you had a good evening?' he asked.

She considered. 'No,' she said. 'Not very.'

He looked at her but obviously didn't want to appear curious, so she said, 'I went with a friend to an operatic society rehearsal. Not really my thing.'

He laughed. 'My mother belonged to one of those. Not really my thing either.'

They drank their wine. 'I'm trying to get up the courage to ask you something,' said Jake.

'You want to borrow some more coffee?'

'More important than that.' He took another sip of his wine and put the glass on the coffee table. 'You can say no — in fact you probably will, but please consider it first.'

'It sounds very serious,' said Lauren, 'but I can't consider it if I don't know what it is.'

Jake took a deep breath. 'Every year, on the birthday of our founder, my company holds a black tie dinner and dance. It's usually very good, but it's best if you have a partner.'

I know what's coming, thought Lauren.

'I wondered … that is, it would be very kind of you if you'd agree to come with me as my partner for the evening. No strings,' he said hastily. 'Just as my partner for the evening.'

Lauren opened her mouth to refuse. How could she go out for such an evening with a man she'd only spoken to twice, to a venue where she wouldn't know anyone?

'Please,' he begged. 'I'd be so grateful.'

'But you must have plenty of friends,' she protested.

'Most of my female friends are part of a couple. Friends of my wife and me.'

'Your wife?'

'Ex-wife. We're divorced.'

'Oh.' Lauren looked at him uncertainly.

'A year ago,' he said. 'She — she found

someone she liked better. Well, actually, an old flame. They reignited.'

Lauren smiled but felt trapped. To gain time she poured them both some more wine. After her resolution not to get involved again, she was being asked out by the new occupant of flat twelve. No, she wouldn't do it.

Jake was looking at her. She felt herself drawn into his intense gaze. Those glowing dark blue eyes beseeching her.

'Yes,' she found herself saying. 'Yes, I'll come with you if I'm free.'

He gave a loud sigh of relief. 'You won't be sorry. You'll get a superb meal and dancing. Do you like dancing?'

Lauren nodded. 'I love it, though I don't get many chances to dance nowadays. I seem to be too busy,' she added hastily, worried he might think she had no one to take her out.

He stood up. 'I'll give you more details nearer the time.'

And I've got just the dress for a posh dinner dance, she thought happily, closing the door behind him.

38

★ ★ ★

Morice's club was packed with excited people when Lauren and Daisy arrived. Waiters balancing trays of drinks twisted and twirled round the too-close tables. The lights were low and Lauren was surprised that Morice was able to spot them as they entered. He waved and conducted them to a table near the stage where the resident band was already in full swing.

'I love the dress,' said Daisy, 'but I thought you were going to wear the green one.'

'I'm keeping that for a special occasion. I've been invited to a company dinner and dance.'

Daisy's eyes widened. 'Invited by whom?'

Lauren coloured slightly, glad the low lights didn't give her away. 'Actually, it's Jake.'

'Well he's a quick worker,' said Daisy.

'I'm only going as his partner for the evening,' Lauren explained. 'He hasn't anyone to take.'

Daisy looked dubious. 'If he's as attractive as you say, I find that hard to believe.'

A tray of drinks appeared on the table and Lauren was glad of the interruption.

The band left the stage. Morice jumped up to introduce the guest artistes for the evening. They were American and enthusiastic. It was their first visit to a British club and they were determined to make their mark. Lauren found their music almost unbearably loud.

Morice rejoined them and brought Ray with him. Morice's face was shining with excitement. 'Aren't they amazing,' he kept saying. 'We were so lucky to get them. They could have gone to Dixie's down the road.'

Ray smiled at Lauren. 'Do you like this sort of music?' he asked quietly.

'Well, I'm sure it's very good,' she said politely, 'but it's so loud.'

'Would you prefer to sit at the bar?' he asked. 'It's right at the back of the room.'

She smiled at him gratefully and stood up. 'Thank you, I would.'

He led the way to the back of the room

and helped her onto the high bar stool. 'What would you like to drink?'

Lauren watched him as he collected drinks for them. He was shorter than her and quite stocky. Not her favourite type of man. But he was quiet and friendly and seemed quite happy to keep her company without trying to impress her.

Perhaps he doesn't fancy me, she thought with amusement. *Perhaps I'm not his type*. She looked up to find him studying her. She flushed a little and took a sip of her drink

'I'm sorry,' he said. 'You must think me very rude staring at you like that.'

'No, no, of course not.' Embarrassed, she looked away to where the American band was performing with undiminished energy.

'It's just that I was trying to get the courage to tell you something.'

She looked at him. He was gazing down at the floor.

'Morice said that you finished with your boyfriend a few months ago,' he began. 'He suggested ... suggested that we might …' He paused. 'This is very difficult.'

'I know what you're going to say,' Lauren interrupted. 'All my girlfriends are trying to find me a new partner. Daisy must have discussed it with Morice, so …' She made a gesture with her hand. 'Don't say any more.'

There was silence for a few minutes, then Ray said, 'I only met Morice a few weeks ago when I joined the band. He doesn't really know anything about me.' He looked straight at her. 'The thing is, I have a partner already. I'm married. My wife lives in America. She's a singer.'

Lauren didn't want to be nosy but she had to ask. 'Why does she live in America and you in England?'

Ray grinned. 'Sounds odd, doesn't it,' he agreed. 'She's a California girl, loves the sun. She lived in England for a year and couldn't stand the weather. So she went back home on the understanding that I'd join her eventually. We see a lot of each other — pop back and forth, you know. We both want to work on our careers, so while we're young, it suits us.'

There was another silence between them, then Lauren gave a little sigh. 'What an interesting arrangement. So now we can just be friends.' She held out a hand and he clasped it warmly.

'Friends,' he echoed, and they picked up their glasses and clinked them together.

'Would you like to dance?' Ray asked. 'I love your dress. You could show it off. It's a shame to hide it here at the back of the room.'

Lauren smiled warmly and slid off her stool. Ray wasn't tall with black curly hair and blue eyes, but he liked her new dress and he didn't want to be her boyfriend. She led the way onto the dance floor and they spent the next fifteen minutes dancing happily.

Lauren caught Daisy's eye. Her friend gave her a thumbs-up signal.

If she means what I think she means, she can forget it, Lauren thought. *Ray and I are just friends, and that's the way it will stay.*

3

'Hello. Off on holiday?' Lauren, returning to her flat after shopping, accosted the tall suitcase-carrying figure emerging from Jake's doorway.

'Wish I was. No, business, I'm afraid. Takes me away occasionally.'

'Where are you going?'

'Cardiff for a week, then Manchester.' Jake picked up the suitcase he'd put down to lock the door. 'Sorry, I must go. Don't forget the dinner dance.'

Lauren watched him stride down the corridor, turn the corner and disappear. Then she turned to open her own door. Suddenly she felt rather flat. Jake would be away for two weeks. She switched on her electric fire and, collapsing into the armchair in front of it, gazed disconsolately at the flickering flames. Two weeks was a long time.

Abruptly she jumped up and went

into the kitchen. What on earth was she doing, mooning over someone she'd met only a few times? *Remember the new resolution*, she told herself. She didn't need a boyfriend. Her only interest was her cake business.

She took a cookery book from the shelf and opened it. She'd had an idea yesterday for a new type of mince pie. This was a good time to try it out.

She sat at the kitchen table flicking through the book. There were several different kinds of mince pies, but nothing like her new idea.

Lauren put on a clean white apron, scrubbed her hands, and began to assemble the ingredients. Into a basin of sweet-smelling kirsch she tumbled a packet of cherries and mixed them well. Then she made a tray of pastry cases. Carefully putting a spoonful of her special mincemeat to the sides of the cases, she filled the centres with kirsch-soaked cherries and topped them with a small circle of marzipan. The smell was intoxicating, rich and spicy. She smiled to herself. These would have to be marketed for grown-ups. Children would hardly appreciate them.

She fastened the lids, brushed them with beaten egg, and popped them into the oven. Then with a cup of coffee, she settled down to wait for them to cook.

A tap at the front door made her jump. Opening it, she was surprised to see her new friend, Ray. He gave her a shy smile and shuffled his feet.

'I hope you don't mind. I got your address from Daisy.'

Lauren opened the door wider. 'Come in. It's lovely to see you.'

He did so, and looked around. 'What a cosy flat. I love all the pictures'.

Lauren led him to a seat by the fire.

'I was feeling a bit low,' he explained. 'It's my night off but I haven't really got anywhere to go. I don't know many people yet, and Jason — he's my cousin; we share a flat …' Lauren nodded. 'Jason's at work.'

'You're welcome at any time,' said Lauren. 'Coffee?'

'Please. What a delicious smell.'

'Actually, you can do something for me in a moment,' she said.

'Of course. Anything.'

'You can try out some new cakes. Give me your opinion.'

He smiled brightly. 'Super! The sort of job I like.'

The pies were ready. Lauren made some fresh coffee and carried in a plate of mince pies. 'Be careful. They're still very hot.'

Ray gave her a pleased smile. 'Am I the first to try them?'

'The very first. And I want an honest opinion. You don't have to be polite.'

Ray took a pie, closed his eyes and didn't speak until he had eaten the lot. Then he opened his eyes and sighed. 'I've never tasted such a wonderful mince pie,' he said. 'What do the books say? Bursting with flavour.'

Lauren, who had been watching him, tried one herself. She nodded. 'I think they'll do.'

'I should say they'll do.' Ray was enthusiastic. 'They're wonderful.'

Lauren sat back in her armchair. It was relaxing to have a male friend who was just a friend, who didn't want anything from her. She smiled at Ray. 'You came at just the right time.'

'D'you often invent new cakes?' he asked.

'Oh yes. Keeps the interest of our regulars. And everyone likes to try something different.'

He stayed for an hour. They chatted idly about the shop and the band and Daisy and Morice.

'You and Daisy are very close, aren't you?' Ray said.

'She's my assistant but also my best friend. She's been with me since the beginning of our venture. I'd be lost without her.'

When Ray stood up to go, Lauren was surprised to see that it was ten o'clock. *And I didn't think of Jake once*, she realised as she closed the front door.

★ ★ ★

On Saturday, she surprised her father by turning up at his restaurant, La Belle Étoile. She was greeted warmly by all the staff.

Do you want to eat in the kitchen or at my table?' her father asked.

'At your table. I don't want to be in the way.' She smiled around at the staff.

'And how is life?' Her father poured her a glass of his best Drapeaux de Floridene and sipped his own appreciatively.

'Life is interesting,' she replied. 'My friends are busy trying to find me a boyfriend and I'm busy foiling them.'

'Ever hear from that Australian?' he asked.

She was saved from answering by the arrival of their first course.

'This looks good,' she said.

'It's a new way of serving smoked salmon.' He picked up his knife and fork. 'Not my idea, alas. Jean-Marc thought of it.'

'I shall compliment him later. It tastes superb.'

The first course was followed by a creamy chicken casserole with baby vegetables.

'Jean-Marc was a find, wasn't he,' said Lauren. 'I'm surprised he isn't in charge of one of your other restaurants.'

'I need him here. When I'm doing a television broadcast I know everything will be perfect with him in charge. You can have the running of La Belle Anna or La Belle Fleur the moment you say the word.' Her father gave her a wicked glance under his eyelashes.

She gave him an exasperated look in return. 'I have my own business,' she said firmly. 'I'm doing well, and I may expand into more shops.'

'Cakes!' he said in mock revulsion. 'What about proper food?'

'I've just created a new mince pie.' Lauren replaced her cutlery neatly on the plate. 'It has a centre filled with Kirsch-soaked cherries and a tiny circle of marzipan under the lid.'

For a moment he looked interested. New ideas in food always captured his imagination. 'Good. Good. How are they going?'

'Well, at the moment only two people

have tried them,' she laughed. 'But I've brought you some. You can tell me what you think. But no featuring them on television! I want them for my shop exclusively.'

Her father returned to the question she'd left unanswered at the start of the meal. 'Do you ever hear from that Australian?'

'I didn't expect to,' she answered.

'Thank goodness. You can do better than him. And I don't want you living on the other side of the world. I want you here where I can see you.' He reached out and took her hand between both of his. 'You're all I've got, Pidge.'

Lauren's mother had died two years ago and her father was finding it hard to get over the loss. She thought it would be wise to lighten the conversation. 'What about your fluffy blondes?' she asked.

He stood up, ignoring the question. 'I'll go and check on the kitchen. Meringues with cream and berries suit you?'

'Perfectly.'

When her father returned to the

table, he was carrying two plates of tiny meringues filled with thick cream and glistening red berries. 'Your favourite, I believe.' He set a plate in front of her.

Lauren looked around the restaurant. It was decorated in shades of green with lamps and ornaments of gold. Waiters glided silently from the kitchen to the tables as though on wheels. The ambience was expensive, like the food, she thought.

'Excuse me for a moment.' Her father left the table to greet two well-dressed ladies who had just come in. He conducted them to a table, chatted for a few minutes, then returned to Lauren.

'Lady Mary Swann and her daughter, an up-and-coming actress,' he explained. 'They often visit.'

Lauren smiled at the self-satisfied expression on his face. She glanced at her watch. 'I'd better go. Early start tomorrow. I'll just say goodbye and thanks to Jean-Marc and the gang.'

On the journey home she thought over the conversation with her father.

He respected her ambition but never stopped trying to recruit her to run one of his restaurants. He would love to have them working together, she knew, but she had her own ideas and she would need a very good reason to abandon them.

★   ★   ★

The new mince pies were a great success. They sold out as fast as Lauren and Daisy could make them. Jake's two weeks away went quickly, and it was soon the night of the dinner dance.

Daisy was very pleased that Lauren had such a glamorous date. She insisted on doing Lauren's hair for her.

'You've got a light touch with hair, like you have with pastry.' Lauren looked with satisfaction at her reflection. 'I like the way you've arranged those side pieces. I can never do them so well.'

'He'll fall for you, no doubt about it,' said Daisy. 'In your new dress, you'll look stunning.'

'I don't want him to fall for me,' said Lauren. 'This isn't a date. I'm just doing him a favour, being his partner for the evening to help him out.'

'Of course. I forgot.' Daisy put on a solemn face. Then she chuckled. 'But I know he'll fall for you.'

When she'd gone, Lauren carefully made up her face and took the green and cream striped dress from its hanger. She covered her hair with a silk scarf to protect Daisy's work and lifted the dress over her head. It slipped into place and with difficulty she fastened the buttons at the back. She should have put on the dress before Daisy left.

At last she was ready. *Quite elegant*, she thought with satisfaction as she gazed at her reflection. *I don't think I'll let him down*.

The admiration in his eyes when she opened the door a few minutes later convinced her that he was more than satisfied with her appearance.

'You look quite beautiful,' he said. 'I shall have a job to keep you to myself this evening.'

Lauren felt the colour rise in her cheeks. She wanted to remind him that she was only his partner for the evening, but she kept silent. If he wanted to introduce a note of romance, she was in the mood to agree. But only for this evening.

'I have a taxi waiting,' he said as she picked up her bag and her short velvet cloak. 'I don't want to worry about parking — or drinking.'

She threw him an anxious glance.

'Don't worry,' he said. 'I shan't disgrace you. I'm not a great drinker.'

The event was being held at the swankiest hotel in the district. Lauren had often passed it but had never been inside. She was keen to see whether the inside matched the elegance of the exterior with its fountains and huge topiary birds.

*   *   *

She was not disappointed. The foyer shone with rich cream paint and gold lamps. Extravagant floral arrangements of cream and bronze chrysanthemums softened the corners of the room and the bends of the wide staircase.

They mounted the stairs and Jake took Lauren to the ladies' cloakroom. She handed her cloak to the attendant and checked her reflection in the cheval mirror, then flushed with pleasure. Even she could see that her appearance was pleasing.

An older lady patting her hair at the mirror caught Lauren's eye and smiled. 'What a beautiful dress,' she said. 'So elegant.'

Lauren flushed. 'Thank you.'

She was still smiling at the compliment when she rejoined Jake. He thought the smile was for him and returned it.

'Come along.' He put an arm gently round her waist. 'This way, I think. We'll follow the noise.'

They stood on the threshold of the ballroom. For a moment Lauren felt a little shy. A room full of laughing, talking, dancing people, and she was sure she knew none of them.

Jake drew her forward. 'Come on. I must introduce you to Mr. Reynolds and his wife.

He's the big cheese. Now smile nicely.'

Mr. Reynolds stood just inside the door waiting for his guests to be introduced. He was tall, stick-thin, and had a bushy moustache. Lauren immediately noticed the lady next to him, obviously his wife.

'Why, here's the young lady with the beautiful dress,' said Mrs. Reynolds with a smile.

Lauren immediately felt less shy. Jake made the introductions and Lauren found Mr. Reynolds to be not at all as dry as he'd seemed.

'I shall expect a turn with you later,' he said to Lauren. 'I always dance with the most attractive young ladies.'

Lauren and Jake joined the dancers on the floor. She fitted perfectly into his arms. He held her firmly but not too tightly, and she was pleased that he didn't show off with fancy steps and moves. She smiled up at him. He looked so handsome in his evening clothes, she felt as proud as if he really did belong to her. The evening was going to be as enjoyable as she had hoped.

As they circled the floor, Jake greeted several people but didn't stop dancing, so Lauren wasn't introduced to anyone. But she was aware of close scrutiny from many people. She lifted her head proudly. She looked as good as anyone else; in fact — she felt wicked thinking it — her dress was prettier than most.

Supper was a buffet, a large and sumptuous one. 'I told you you'd eat well,' said Jake. 'Come on, let's start this end.'

There were plates of cold meat, pies, pizzas and tiny vol-au-vents. Lauren didn't know where to start. In the middle section of the long table were curries and hot savoury dishes for those who wanted something more substantial. She admired the salad table with its bowls of bright red and green salads, many heavy with fruit in the American fashion.

She cast a professional eye over the puddings and cakes on a separate table, looking for inspiration. Perhaps she'd try a few later.

They turned away from the table with their loaded plates and were hailed by a

58

couple seated at a small corner table. 'Jake, over here,' called a tall, fair young man.

'Steven Page,' said Jake. 'He has the desk next to mine. He's okay. You'll like him.' They joined Steven and his wife, Zoe, a pretty young woman as dark as Steven was fair. Lauren was introduced as an old friend of Jake's.

'I love your dress,' said Zoe.

Lauren glowed. Another compliment. She felt the evening couldn't be better.

Coffee was being served at a table at the far end of the long dining room. As they joined the queue, a striking-looking redhead in a bronze-coloured dress moved in front of Jake.

'Hello, Jake.' Her voice was soft and purring. 'I didn't expect to see you here on your own.'

'Hello, Pamela.' His voice was expressionless, and Lauren didn't think he was pleased to see the other woman. 'I'm not alone. I'm with a friend.' He put an arm round Lauren.

The redhead's eyes narrowed. 'Well aren't you going to introduce us?'

'Lauren, this is Pamela. She's one of the secretaries. Pamela, this is Lauren.'

An introduction and nothing else, thought Lauren. The women exchanged brief smiles.

Lauren and Jake had reached the table, and while they collected their cups of coffee, Pamela disappeared. Jake looked relieved. Lauren longed to ask him about the other woman but didn't want to pry. His private life was no concern of hers.

'When we've drunk this, let's go and dance some more,' said Jake. 'We dance well together, don't you think?'

Lauren smiled at him. It was true, they did dance well together. Their bodies fitted comfortably, their steps matched, and they moved in harmony to the music. Despite her initial doubts, she found she was really enjoying the evening.

'Thank you again for coming with me,' he said. 'It's been more fun than I'd imagined.'

Lauren placed her cup on the nearest table. 'I'll just go to the ladies' room and freshen up while you finish your coffee,' she said.

In the cloakroom she was not pleased to see that the only occupant was the red-headed Pamela. She gave her a quick smile of acknowledgement and went to the mirror, taking a lipstick from her bag as she did so.

'How long have you known Jake?' Pamela asked.

'Just a few weeks.' Lauren applied the lipstick and replaced it in her bag.

'He and I were an item once,' said Pamela.

Lauren gave her another tight smile. She wished the woman would go.

'Are you two serious about each other?'

'I'm sorry; I don't think it's any of your business.' Lauren began to wash her hands.

Pamela gave her a furious look and moved to the hand basin. She turned on the cold tap, and before Lauren realised what she was doing, pressed her thumb against the base of the tap and directed the water towards Lauren. The cold stream struck her full in the face and poured downwards to soak her dress.

'Oh!' Lauren jumped backwards as two women came into the cloakroom.

'I'm so sorry.' Pamela rushed forward with a handful of tissues grabbed from a box on the table. 'How careless of me.'

The two women tried to dry off Lauren's dress with more tissues as Pamela continued to apologise.

'My finger got caught in the tap,' she said unconvincingly. 'I don't know how it happened.'

'You poor thing,' said one of the women to Lauren. 'Your dress is soaked. These tissues haven't done much good. Perhaps we could get a towel from reception.'

'Please don't bother,' said Lauren. 'I'll find my friend and ask him to take me home.' She turned to Pamela. 'And please stop apologising,' she said. 'We both know you did it deliberately.'

The door slammed behind her as she hurried out into the corridor. Jake was waiting at the end. 'What on earth ...' he began.

'Please take me home.' Lauren was close to tears — tears of rage and disappointment.

'But what happened? You're soaking wet.'

'Can we go home?' begged Lauren.

'I'll get your wrap.' He darted off. He was soon back, tucked the cloak round Lauren's shoulders and led her to the front door. 'Wait here. I'll phone for a taxi.'

'No. I'll come with you.' She didn't want to see Pamela again.

'Come along then,' said Jake. 'Let's hurry.'

Luckily the taxi firm wasn't far away. The driver switched on the heater. Even though warmth was flooding the vehicle, Lauren began to shiver. The cold, wet dress clung to her. She longed to get it off.

As they drove out of the car park and into the main road, Jake turned to her. 'Now then, what happened?' he demanded. 'I don't believe it was an accident.'

Lauren was silent for a few seconds, thinking. Should she tell him? But why not? She owed Pamela nothing. Quite the opposite.

'It was Pamela,' she said. 'She did it quite deliberately.'

'Threw water at you?'

Lauren nodded. 'She asked if we were serious about each other, then she put her thumb below the tap and directed the water straight at me.'

Jake said nothing at first, then sighed. 'Lauren, I'm so sorry,' he said. 'Pamela's good at her job, but I think she's unbalanced. I went out with her for a while before I was married. But there was something ... I don't know ... *odd* about her. I finished the relationship and she wasn't pleased.

'She hated my wife,' he continued. 'I don't think Marilyn ever did anything to her, but Pamela was always making snide remarks about her. And she was so pleased when we divorced. Perhaps she thought she and I would get together again. Seeing you and me together must have made her realise I wouldn't go back to her.'

They'd reached the flats. The driver pulled in near to the door.

'You go straight up.' Jake opened the car door for her. 'Get out of that wet dress. I'll pay the driver and be with you in a moment.'

Still shivering, Lauren didn't stop to argue. In a few minutes she was in her warm flat and snuggling into her cosy dressing gown.

Jake knocked at the door and she got up to let him in.

'Lauren, I can't apologise enough. What an ending to our pleasant evening.'

'It wasn't your fault.' Lauren felt better now that she was out of the uncomfortable wet dress. 'I think I'll make some drinking chocolate. Would you like some?'

They sat either side of the fire clutching mugs of hot drinking chocolate. Suddenly, Lauren gave a sneeze.

'Please don't get a cold.' Jake bent and turned the fire up a notch. 'I shall feel so guilty. Perhaps you'd better go straight to bed.'

Lauren stood up. 'You're right. And as

it's Sunday tomorrow, I can have a lie-in.'

At the door, Jake put his hands on her shoulders and kissed her cheek. 'I enjoyed the evening. Thank you again for coming with me and looking so beautiful. And ...'

Lauren shook her head. 'Don't apologise any more. I enjoyed the evening too. Thank you for taking me.'

She put her wet dress on a hanger and hung it in the bathroom to dry. Hopefully it wouldn't suffer from its wetting, as the water had been clean.

She gave her reflection in the mirror a rueful smile. *Pride goes before a fall.* It was her punishment for feeling so proud of the compliments on her appearance.

4

'Surely you've heard of speed dating.' Claire took the box of cakes Lauren handed her and stowed them carefully in her shopping bag.

'I've heard of it.' Lauren took the money for the cakes. 'I thought it was popular a few years ago. They don't do it now, surely.'

'You know this town,' laughed Claire. 'Always years behind everywhere else. Anyway, there's a session on Thursday in the pub next to the library. Would you like to come with me?'

'What about Joe?' Claire had an on/off relationship with a teacher at her son's school. Obviously at the moment it was off.

Claire tossed her head. 'Joe doesn't own me. Speed dating sounds fun. What about it — will you come?'

'I've told you all —' Lauren began.

'I know. You're not looking for a man. Well, just come for the experience. You don't have to commit yourself.'

Daisy finished serving her customer and came over. She had been listening to the exchange. 'Go on, Lauren,' she urged. 'It'll be something different.'

Lauren gave in. 'Oh all right. But only this once. And I'm not committing myself.'

Claire waved. 'See you on Thursday. Half past seven on the library steps.'

As Claire left the shop, Lauren made a face at Daisy. 'You lot don't give up, do you? This is a put-up job. Claire isn't looking for someone else, is she?'

Daisy picked up an empty cake tray and carried it into the kitchen. 'Me, I only know what I'm told,' she called back over her shoulder, 'and I ain't been told nothing.'

'Very funny,' said Lauren. She filled a bucket with hot water, ready to mop the floor. 'Are you busy this evening?'

'No. Why?'

'Can you come home with me? I've got an idea I want to discuss. You'll have to take pot luck with the meal, but I think you'll like my idea.'

★ ★ ★

Lauren put together a scratch meal of pork pie, cheese and tomatoes, and hot rolls. Daisy was anxious to hear the new idea, but Lauren made her wait until they'd finished eating and cleared the table. Then she brought out some pads of drawing paper and packets of coloured pencils. They sometimes used these when planning designs on cakes.

Daisy turned a puzzled face towards her. 'More cake patterns?'

'No. Biscuits.'

'We don't make biscuits.'

'We're going to start. I tried some homemade biscuits at a craft fair at the weekend. They were delicious and very popular.'

'Won't they take up a lot of our time?'

'No. I'll find time. I'll make them and you'll decorate them.'

'Me?' Daisy's eyes opened wide.

'Of course you. You're the artistic one. Look at the beautiful cards you make.'

Daisy seldom bought a birthday card; she took pride in designing her own. Her friends treasured the exquisitely coloured cards if they were lucky enough to receive one.

'This is a good time to try a new idea. It will be Christmas in a few months. Boxes of homemade biscuits will be something different. Ideal for presents.'

Daisy put an elbow on the table and rested her chin on her hand, thinking. Lauren watched her.

'Well come on,' she urged after a few minutes, 'tell me what you think. Is it a good idea?'

Daisy sat up. 'It's a good idea if we can find the time. But don't forget, you want to make more of your new mince pies for Christmas.'

'I've thought about that,' said Lauren. 'We'll take on an assistant, and you can spend more time with the biscuits.'

'Can we afford an assistant?'

'Let me worry about that. Are you

willing to commit to the new venture?'

Daisy gave a wide grin. 'Sounds fun. Of course I'm willing.'

Lauren pushed a pad across the table. 'Let's try a few ideas. I thought solid blocks of colour like stained glass windows.'

Daisy picked up a pencil. 'For Christmas we want to try something like this.' She sketched rapidly and pushed the pad back to Lauren. She had drawn an angel, a Christmas tree and a Father Christmas. She pulled the pad back again.

'We'll need some really good food colouring to decorate them. Something like this. They need to glow with jewel colours.' Rapidly she added colour to each sketch.

Lauren studied the page. 'If you can do something like this, we're on to a winner,' she declared. 'It'll be a lot of work.'

Daisy sat back, looking satisfied. 'I'll get onto the internet this evening and see where I can get really good colouring and decorations,' she said, standing up.

Lauren went into the kitchen and returned with a bottle and two glasses. She poured them each an inch of wine.

'I know you're driving,' she silenced Daisy's protests. 'This is only a mouthful to toast our new idea.' They raised their glasses.

'To our biscuits,' said Daisy.

'May they be a fantastic success,' said Lauren.

* * *

Lauren placed an advertisement for an assistant in an agency window first thing the next morning. At two o'clock, a beautiful blonde girl appeared in the shop.

'You want assistant,' she said to Lauren. 'I see notice in window.'

'Yes, but I expected a written application,' said Lauren, flustered to be rushed like this.

'Written app … Oh you want me to write what I can do?'

'Well, yes, it's usual.'

'For me — no. My English is not that

good. But I am learning fast. I go to English classes.'

Lauren looked at the woman. Bright blue eyes stared hopefully back at her. Her golden hair was like spun silk. She looks like a fairy princess, thought Lauren. Perhaps her looks would attract more customers.

'What's your name?' she asked.

'Paulina. I am Polish, but I think you guess that already.'

Lauren made up her mind. She lifted the partition in the counter and gestured for Paulina to come through.

'You must speak to my business partner, Daisy. If she's happy with you ...'

They went through to the kitchen. 'Daisy, this is Paulina. She'd like to be our new assistant. Will you talk to her?'

When Daisy and Paulina returned to the shop, the latter was smiling happily.

'I think Paulina would be an asset to our business.' Daisy was looking pleased. 'Her aunt and uncle run a small café and shop in Cracow. She often helped out, so she's used to dealing with customers.'

'We'll give you a month's trial,' Lauren decided. 'Be here tomorrow morning at eight.'

After a short discussion about wages and uniform, the young Polish woman left and Lauren and Daisy smiled at each other.

'You'd better keep her away from your father,' said Daisy. 'She's just the sort he likes for an assistant on his TV show. He'll steal her.'

Lauren looked thoughtful. 'If she's interested, we might let him have her occasionally,' she mused. 'It'd be a little reward for her. And possibly publicity for us.'

'You don't miss a trick, do you? Come and see the other designs I've drawn.' Daisy led the way to the kitchen.

* * *

Lauren was on the library steps in good time on Thursday. She looked around. Where was Claire?

A tinkling tune came from her

handbag. She groped among the contents for her mobile phone.

'Lauren — look, I'm dreadfully sorry but I can't make it. Something's come up.'

'What d'you mean? Couldn't you have let me know before this?'

Claire ignored the question. 'My baby-sitter has let me down,' she said. 'She's got a bad toothache. I'm dreadfully sorry. What will you do? Will you go on your own?'

'Certainly not. I was only going because of you. See you sometime. And don't come up with any more bright ideas.' She switched off the mobile and thrust it back into her bag. She had a horrible suspicion that Claire was making an excuse. It was quite likely that Joe had put pressure on her.

All dressed up and nowhere to go, she thought. *I could go to the cinema. Or just go home.*

A voice behind her made her spin round. 'Lauren. Are you waiting for someone?'

It was Jake. Thoughts began to buzz

in her head. If she said yes, he would probably wait with her. If she said no, he might see that as an excuse to invite her out. She didn't want him to think she had nowhere to go, or worse, that she'd been stood up.

She looked up at the library. CONVERSATIONAL FRENCH said a notice. COME AND LEARN ENOUGH FRENCH FOR YOUR HOLIDAY.

She gestured vaguely in the direction of the notice. 'I was … I was making up my mind whether to join that class.'

'It starts at seven thirty and it's almost that now. Come along. We'd better hurry.'

'We? D'you mean you want to learn French too?'

He grinned down at her. 'Why not? I've forgotten most of what I learned at school. We can help each other.' He put a hand under her elbow and hurried her up the steps.

They were just in time. A slightly harassed-looking young woman was calling twenty or so people to order. 'Come along everyone. We must make a start.'

Lauren was pleased to hear a French accent. She didn't want to be taught by an English person. She and Jake crept into the back row and slid into seats behind a small table.

'Can you lend me some paper to take notes?' he whispered.

'I haven't any. I was going to ask you.'

'You were going to join an evening class without even a notebook?'

She looked at him. 'What about you?'

He looked at a loss then said feebly, 'I — er — rushed out without it.'

An efficient-looking young woman in front of them was opening a large binder. Jake leaned forward and whispered to her. She handed him two blank sheets of paper.

'Here we are.' He handed one to Lauren. 'Now we're ready.'

'*Bonsoir, tout le monde*,' said the young teacher. '*Mon nom est* Mademoiselle Royale. Good evening everyone. My name is Miss Royale. Now I should like to know your names. Say '*Mon nom est*' and then your name.'

In turn the members of the class gave

77

their names. 'I feel about seven,' whispered Jake.

The class continued. The teacher was efficient and didn't make anyone feel embarrassed. Lauren found she was enjoying herself.

The time went quickly. Worksheets were handed out to be completed at home and brought next week.

'Will you help me with my homework?' asked Jake.

Lauren glanced down at the sheet. 'If you can't manage this, you shouldn't be here,' she said severely.

He smiled. She studied him. He had a lovely smile. His eyes crinkled at the corners and his mouth pouted slightly.

'I don't believe you intended to come to this French class,' she said.

He looked at her under his eyelashes. 'If I'm perfectly truthful, I have my doubts about you.'

Lauren folded her homework and put it in her handbag. All around them people were preparing to leave the room. Lauren glanced at her watch.

'Nine o'clock. I'm going home.'

Jake followed her from the room. 'Nine o'clock is early,' he protested. 'You can't go home yet. Let's go for a drink.' He put out a hand and caught her arm. 'Please, Lauren. I don't want to go home yet.'

'You don't want to go home yet,' she repeated. 'Well, I have an early start to-morrow. I don't want to go home late.'

'We won't,' he wheedled. 'Come on. Just for an hour.' He hurried her down the steps and along the street to the lighted windows of a pub, once an old coaching inn: the Old Grey Mare. The inside was cosy with dark wood, two open fires and many nooks and crannies. He guided her to a seat at a table behind a wooden screen.

The room was hot. Lauren slipped off her coat. Jake looked pleased. *He thinks that means I intend to stay*, she thought.

'Are you hungry?' he asked.

She thought for a moment. 'Actually, I am. I didn't have time for an evening meal.'

They studied the menu. 'What about roast pork sandwiches?' he asked. 'Or would you prefer salad?'

'Roast pork sounds lovely. Thank you.'

'And to drink? Wine? Or would cider go better with pork?'

'Cider will be fine. Thank you.'

They didn't have to wait long, and were soon tucking into pork sandwiches with tasty stuffing.

'I like a lady who can handle a sandwich,' Jake said with a smile. 'My wife — my ex-wife — never eats bread. It's difficult to enjoy a sandwich when the person opposite only eats the filling.'

'I'm afraid I have what's called a healthy appetite.' Lauren picked up the second half of her sandwich. 'I enjoy my food.'

He studied her. 'For a person who enjoys her food and makes cakes for a living, and no doubt tastes them, you are remarkably slim.'

'Metabolism,' she said cheerfully. 'I never put on weight. I don't sit down much in the day, and on Sundays I go for walks if I can, so the calories don't have a chance to stick.'

'We must go for a walk together sometime,' he suggested.

Lauren concentrated on her sandwich and made no reply. If they did too many things together they'd become a couple, which would please her friends but go against her resolve. Her business must come first.

She realised that Jake was asking her a question. She looked up. 'I'm sorry. I was thinking.'

'I asked if you would allow me a personal question.'

'Well yes, I suppose so.'

'How is it that an attractive girl like you has no boyfriend?'

'There was someone,' she began slowly. 'We were in a relationship for a year.' She sighed. 'I thought it meant more to him than it did.'

'You broke up?'

'He returned to Australia. He'd only intended to be here for a year or so. I knew that from the start, but I suppose I thought our feelings for each other would overcome his desire to return home. Of course, they didn't.'

'And there's been no one else?'

'I don't want anyone else,' she retorted fiercely. 'All my energies are for my business now. I want to really build it up. Perhaps open more shops.'

'Good for you.' He picked up their glasses. 'Just one refill?'

She nodded. 'Then we must go.'

He returned with the drinks and settled himself in his chair again.

'And what about you?' asked Lauren.

'You mean, why am I living alone in a flat?'

'Mmm ...'

'I was married for eight years — happily, I believed. Then Marilyn, my wife, began to take an interest in certain websites on the computer, the ones that find old flames. Like I told you, the rest is history. She left, taking my son with her.'

'You have a child?' Lauren was surprised. He didn't seem like a father. 'But you see your son?' she asked anxiously. She hated the thought of children deprived of a parent by the selfish actions of adults.

'Oh yes. They don't live far away. I can have him whenever I like for outings and so on. It's not the same as living with him, but … I suppose I'm lucky. Some wives are very difficult about access.'

'How old is he, and what's his name? Tell me about him.'

'His name's Alfi. He's six and a half years old. He's supposed to look like me, but he has fair hair like his mum.'

'I should like to meet him,' said Lauren. 'I love children, especially little boys.'

Jake reached into his pocket, brought out a wallet, and extracted a photograph. He handed it to her.

She looked at the little boy. He was like Jake, curly hair and blue eyes, but his hair bubbled up in blonde curls. 'He's cute,' she said warmly.

'The next time he visits I'll bring him over to see you.'

They finished their drinks in silence, each busy with their thoughts. Then Lauren glanced at her watch.

'Goodness, look at the time.' She picked up her bag. 'I really must go.'

It wasn't far to the flats. They strolled back in companionable silence. Jake slipped an arm round her waist. Lauren felt too tired to protest.

'Stairs or lift?'

'Lift. I have no energy left for stairs.'

He pressed the button and the door opened. 'I have to get something from my car,' he said. 'I've enjoyed this evening. Shall we do our homework together tomorrow?'

The door closed before she could answer. Lauren smiled at her reflection in the mirror. All in all, it had been an enjoyable evening. And she had learned a great deal about her new neighbour.

5

Paulina arrived early next morning wearing a neat black skirt and a black jumper. From her bag she took a small frilly white apron which she fastened to her jumper with a tiny brooch.

'I sit up late to make this,' she said with pride, gesturing to the apron. 'Is suitable?'

'Very suitable,' said Lauren, 'and very pretty. You're artistic, I see.'

'Art …? Oh — like artist. Yes, I am artist. I like to draw and paint.'

Lauren set her to work arranging trays of cakes. Soon customers began to arrive, and the new pretty assistant was a great success.

'I think we can have a coffee in peace today,' said Lauren, 'and leave the shop to Paulina.'

'How was the speed dating?' asked Daisy. 'Did you meet any nice young men?'

'Wait till I see Claire,' said Lauren, and

she told Daisy all about the night before.

'Well if she'd turned up, you wouldn't have spent the evening with Jake,' Daisy pointed out reasonably.

'And I shouldn't have discovered that he was married for eight years and has a son.'

Daisy looked at her. 'Does it matter?'

'Matter? That he's been married and has a son? Of course not. He's nothing to me other than a pleasant neighbour.' She stood up and took their cups to the sink.

'Did he kiss you goodnight?' Daisy asked mischievously.

'He did not. Now go and send Paulina through for her coffee.' Lauren dried the cups and poured more coffee, muttering to herself, 'Kiss me indeed.'

Paulina came in. 'I'm sorry, did you say something to me?'

'No, Paulina. I'm just talking to myself.' She passed over the cup of coffee. 'Take a cake if you'd like one. How are you enjoying your first day?'

They chatted for a few minutes, then Lauren took a bag of change through to the shop. It was empty of customers. Daisy was wiping down the counters.

'It was a good idea getting an assistant, don't you think?' Lauren placed the change in the till.

'She'll be fine, but we'll have to increase sales to pay for her wages.'

'We will. We'll start on the biscuits next week.'

'Good. I'm looking forward to it,' said Daisy.

'I don't suppose you and Morice are free on Saturday evening, are you?'

'Morice is never free on Saturdays, and this week I've promised to go to the club to hear his new girl singer. Why?'

'I'm having a little dinner party,' said Lauren. 'I thought it'd be nice for Paulina to meet some of our friends. I particularly wanted you and Morice to be there, but I supposed it'd be difficult.'

'Is Jake invited?'

Lauren flushed. 'Of course. He counts as a friend, if nothing else.'

Paulina was thrilled to be invited. 'I have a new dress — ice blue. I shall wear

87

that,' she said delightedly.

And the rest of us needn't make any effort, thought Lauren. *Ice-blue dress and golden hair, she'll be the star of the show*. And yet she didn't feel any jealousy. Paulina was such a sweet young woman and such a willing worker, she deserved some attention.

★   ★   ★

Jake was pleased to receive his invitation. Somehow he misunderstood and seemed to think it would be just the two of them. There wasn't time to correct him, as he was on his way out to see a client.

Lauren watched him disappear round the end of the corridor. Just the two of them. Was that an idea for the future?

She invited Ray to make the numbers even. The other two guests were Judy and her twin brother, Colin, old friends who had started school on the same day as Lauren.

They arrived first, and when Jake appeared, were sitting on the couch with Lauren laughing at some old photographs.

Introductions were made; Jake handed her a large box of chocolates and gave her a quizzical look. *So he* did *think it would be just the two of us*, she mused, accepting the chocolates.

Before they could start a conversation, Ray knocked on the door, and then a few minutes later Paulina made an entrance in her ice-blue dress and little white fur wrap. She looked ravishing. Lauren saw Jake's eyes widen as he was introduced to the Polish woman. He took her hand, made a little bow, and said something that was quite incomprehensible to most of the party.

Paulina clapped her hands. 'Oh, you speak Polish,' she said delightedly.

He shook his head regretfully. 'I'm afraid that 'How do you do, my name is Jake' is the extent of my Polish,' he said to general laughter. The mirth had broken the ice, and Lauren knew that her dinner party would be a success.

Prawn cocktails were waiting for them

on the beautifully decorated table. Then they moved on to tender asparagus with melted butter.

'We don't need to dine at the Ritz,' laughed Colin. 'We can eat as well here.'

Lauren brought in the main course of grilled lamb cutlets with duchesse potatoes, mushrooms and watercress. She was pleased to see Jake eye her appreciatively.

'Where did you learn to cook like this?' he asked.

Colin and Judy burst out laughing. 'Don't you know who her father is?' asked Judy.

Jake looked puzzled. 'Her father?'

'Elvin Tate,' they chorused together.

'Elvin …? Oh, I see. Elvin Tate the TV chef.' Jake looked at Lauren with respect. 'No wonder you can cook. My mother is a terrific fan. Never misses a show.'

A feather-light lemon meringue completed the meal. Lauren was surprised and delighted when Paulina accepted a second helping. With her size ten figure and tiny waist, she looked as if she existed on water and air like a flower.

'I don't think I've had such a delicious meal for ages,' said Jake. 'Round of applause for the chef.'

Embarrassed but happy, Lauren stood up. 'Coffee everyone?'

Judy got to her feet. 'You sit down; I'll make it. I know where everything is. You've done enough.'

She made for the kitchen, and Lauren obediently sat and enjoyed the conversation. Colin had asked Paulina about holiday resorts in Poland. Jake, who had visited the country, joined in.

Lauren sat back and observed her guests. Ray was as quiet as usual but the others were talking animatedly. If she had really been interested in Jake, she might have been jealous of the attention he was giving Paulina. But the younger woman looked so bright and pretty that the admiration on the faces of Jake and Colin was only to be expected.

Judy had just entered with a tray of coffee when the telephone rang. Murmuring excuses, Lauren went into the bedroom and picked up the receiver. It was Morice.

'Lauren, something dreadful has happened,' he began as soon as she answered. 'It's Daisy.'

'What is it? I thought she was with you at the club.'

'She is. Was. We're at her house now. We've been at the accident and emergency department at the hospital for ages.'

'Tell me what happened.'

'We'd just entered the ballroom — she'd been with me in the band room — when her heel skidded on a shiny bit of floor. She put out her hand to save herself as she fell and broke her wrist. Her right one,' he added mournfully. 'Oh Lauren, I'm so sorry. She won't be able to do anything for weeks.'

Lauren was silent, the implications of the accident becoming apparent.

'Lauren, are you still there?'

'Yes, I'm here. How is Daisy now?'

'She's asleep,' he said. 'They gave her some tranquilisers. I don't know whether she was more upset by the pain or by letting you down. You were just going to start the biscuits, weren't you? She can't do anything with a broken wrist.'

'Tell her not to worry. We'll work something out. I'll speak to her in the morning. Don't forget, Morice, to tell her not to worry.'

Easier said than done, she thought as she went back to the others. Now what were they to do?

'Bad news?' asked Jake, looking at her worried face. 'Can we help?'

She sat down and accepted a cup of coffee as she told them about the phone call. 'We were going to start a new project, decorated biscuits, next week. Daisy was to do the decorating. She's right-handed and it's her right wrist, so she's out of cake-making for weeks.'

She sipped her coffee. One phone call and her triumphant evening had turned to ashes. Poor Daisy must be feeling wretched, but not as bad as Lauren herself was feeling. Christmas would be a nightmare without Daisy's help, and the biscuits would have to be put off until next Christmas.

Ray was looking thoughtful. 'Lauren,' he began quietly, 'your problem is not the new biscuit project, it's someone to help you with the day-to-day cake-making. Is that right?'

'It certainly is. Daisy makes half the cakes we sell. Some of them are her speciality. I'll have to advertise, but I don't know how quickly I'll be able to find someone suitable.'

'This might not work out — he might not be interested — but my cousin Jason is looking for a new position. He's been made redundant.'

Lauren's face brightened. 'That could be the solution,' she began. Then a thought struck her. 'But Jason's a chef, isn't he? Would he be interested in just making cakes?'

Ray smiled. 'We don't know until we ask him. I'll get him to ring you in the morning.'

* * *

Jason did better than that. He appeared at eight o'clock as Lauren and Paulina were preparing the shop for opening. Lauren wasn't sure what she was expecting; probably a small, quiet person like Ray. But Jason was tall, fair-haired and very handsome. Lauren noticed Paulina giving him some interested sideways peeps when she thought he wasn't looking. *I shall have to have a quiet word with her*, thought Lauren.

'Ray said you need someone to make cakes for you for a few weeks,' he said after introducing himself.

'We certainly do. But I understand you're a chef. Would making cakes satisfy you?'

Jason took the cup of coffee Paulina had made him and she blushed as he gave her a warm smile. 'I think it would make a nice change,' he said, 'just for a few weeks. I've been offered something for after Christmas. This would fill in nicely till then.'

'I'm sure we can come to an arrangement over pay and hours,' said Lauren. 'Could you start straight away?'

'This very minute. Find me an apron.'

The three of them worked very well together. Lauren was pleased that Jason only needed to be told once when she instructed him. Tray after tray of cupcakes, meringues, gingerbread and shortcake, all even and beautifully risen, appeared from the oven, and Lauren and Paulina were kept busy adding cream or icing and decorations to each cake.

Paulina was full of admiration. 'He is very good cook, for a man,' she kept repeating until Lauren said, 'Paulina, most of the best chefs in the world have been men.'

'Oh I know about them,' Paulina brushed the great chefs aside, 'but not ordinary men.'

Lauren wondered how Jason would feel about being called an ordinary man. The chefs she had known thought of themselves as extraordinary.

At last the day was finished. The shop had been tidied and the kitchen surfaces scrubbed. They left together, and Lauren smiled up at Jason. 'I can't thank you enough. I think you've saved the day.'

He gave her a warm smile in return. 'I've enjoyed it. See you tomorrow. Paulina, are you going this way? Shall we walk together?'

When she reached her flat, Lauren decided to phone Daisy before preparing her evening meal. A very woebegone Daisy answered.

'Lauren, I don't know what to say. I've let you down dreadfully.'

'Nonsense, Daisy,' Lauren said brightly. 'I don't suppose you tried to get a broken wrist. How is it?'

'Very painful. They've strapped it up and I'm on painkillers. But it still hurts. How did you manage today?'

'I'm ringing to tell you not to worry. Guess who's stepping in for a few weeks until you come back?'

There was a pause as Daisy thought. 'I can't imagine,' she said at last. 'Tell me.'

'Jason.'

'Ray's Jason?'

'Ray's Jason,' Lauren repeated.

'But he's a chef.'

'I know, but he's between jobs and happy to fill in to help us out.'

'How marvellous. I feel much happier now.'

'So is Paulina,' said Lauren with a laugh. 'She's really taken with him.'

'She'll work even harder to please him too,' said Daisy. 'And what about the biscuits? Oh dear, I'm beginning to feel bad again.'

'Just concentrate on getting that wrist better,' said Lauren. 'I'll pop in and see you as soon as I can.'

They chatted for a few moments longer, then Lauren said goodbye. She was hungry and wanted her evening meal.

She was eating and going over her dinner party the night before when a thought struck her. French class. Did Jake really want to go again? Did she? Neither of them had set out that evening to attend a French class. But it had been fun. She'd enjoyed the evening. Perhaps she'd pop over to see him later on.

As she was washing up her dinner dishes, there was a knock at the door. Opening it, she found Jake grinning at her over a pile of books.

'French homework,' he said.

'Two minds with a single thought.' Lauren opened the door wider. 'I was going to come over and see you. Do you *want* to go to French classes?'

'Want to go? Of course. Why not?

'Well we didn't intend to join the class, did we?'

'No, but we've started so we'll finish.' He laid the books out on the table. 'I've also got a CD and a DVD about Paris. Should help us. Bought them today. You said you'd help me with my homework,' he reminded her.

'You don't need help. It's very basic.'

'But won't it be more fun to do it together?'

Lauren looked at him. He gave her his cheeky grin. 'We can take it in turns to be teacher,' he said.

'Are you going to take this seriously? I

don't want to waste my time.'

He drew his hand down his face to wipe away the smile. 'Very seriously,' he said. 'We'll aim to be the best pupils in the class.'

They sat at the table and spread out their books and their homework.

'We'll watch the little film when we have a break,' Jake decided.

'How long is all this going to take? I have cakes to make.'

'What about your new cake maker? Can't he do them?'

'Not all of them. You have no idea how many we sell. I make a couple of boxes here most nights and take them in early to decorate.'

'I liked your Paulina,' he said.

'So I noticed,' Lauren said coolly. Then, worried that he might think her jealous, she said, 'She's very pretty, and a good worker. We're lucky to have her.'

Jake picked up his homework sheet. 'This isn't going to tax us. I remember most of it from school.'

'Revision is useful,' said Lauren.

'Shows us where the gaps are in our knowledge. We'll take it in turns. I'll start. *Bonjour.* That's hello.'

'*Bonsoir.* Good evening,' he said.

'*Au revoir.* Goodbye.'

They worked hard for twenty minutes, then laid down their worksheets and smiled at each other.

'It's strange how things come back to you,' said Lauren.

'Yes. I feel quite pleased. We probably know more than we think.'

'I'll make us a coffee.' Lauren stood up. 'You fix up the DVD and we'll watch the film.' She went into the kitchen and was soon back with two mugs of coffee and a plate of biscuits.

'Not homemade?' Jake sounded disappointed.

'You'll have to wait for those. Daisy's accident has put a puncture in that particular wheel.'

'Perhaps Jason is good at biscuits,' Jake suggested.

'But Daisy was going to decorate them. She's very artistic. She'd planned some lovely designs.'

'What about you?'

Lauren looked thoughtful. 'I could try,' she said at last. 'But they wouldn't look like Daisy's. No, we'll leave that idea until next year and hope no one in town thinks of it too.'

Jake finished his coffee. 'Things have a way of working out,' he said, picking up the tray and carrying it into the kitchen.

Lauren looked up as he came back into the room. 'We haven't watched the film. Too busy talking.'

'Never mind. I'll bring them next time.' Jake gathered his books together. 'I've enjoyed this evening.'

'We haven't done much,' said Lauren.

'Exactly. It's been very relaxing. The sort of evening I like.'

Me too, thought Lauren as she locked the door behind him. *And if we continue with our French classes, there'll be many more like it.*

6

Going for a drink and a sandwich had become a routine after French class. Jake even held Lauren's hand as they walked to the Old Grey Mare.

'This is platonic hand-holding,' he said when he caught her looking at him sideways.

'Of course,' she agreed. But she was beginning to find a strange comfort in the warmth of his hand. This alarmed her when she stopped to think about it. Where was her resolve to be a free woman with no romantic attachments?

Sometimes she wondered whether he went out with other women. She'd never seen anyone like that leave his flat, but he could meet them away from home. And did she care? They'd both made their positions clear when they first met. She wanted to concentrate on her business; he wanted some freedom after eight years of matrimony. Friends, that was what they were. Just mates.

She studied his dark curly hair, his straight nose and sensual lips as he read the menu across the table from her. He was so attractive. She hoped she could stick to her resolve and not weaken.

'I said, are you free on Sunday? You're miles away. What are you thinking?'

'Oh, nothing.' Confused, she brushed back her hair. 'I'm sorry. Sunday? Yes, I'm free. Why?'

'I was thinking of going to see my mother. She lives near the sea, and if it's a fine day it'll be a pleasant trip. I wondered whether you'd like to come with me.'

Go to see his mother. Years ago that meant something serious. She looked at him doubtfully.

He seemed to read her mind. 'I've told Mother about my friend and neighbour, Lauren. She understands our relationship.'

She thought for a moment longer. 'Thank you. A day at the seaside would be a nice break.'

He nodded. 'Good.' He replaced the menu on its stand. 'Why do I always look at this? We have the same thing every week. I'll go and order.'

While he was at the bar, Lauren went over her conversation with Daisy last night. She'd called in to see how Daisy's wrist was progressing. Her friend was still strapped up but looking happier.

'It doesn't hurt so much now,' she'd said, 'but I can't do much in the house. I feel so guilty.'

Lauren had made a pot of tea and poured them each a cup. Then she unpacked a box of cakes she'd brought with her.

'I really miss these.' Daisy sank her gleaming white teeth into a pineapple cream.

'You'll soon be making them yourself,' said Lauren. 'Just a few more weeks, I expect.'

Daisy put down her cake and looked serious. 'Lauren, I must tell you something now. It wouldn't be right to spring it on you later.'

'Tell me what?'

'Morice is negotiating a contract to work a year — possibly more — in America.'

'America!' Lauren stared at her. 'What about you?'

'If it happens, I would go too, of course.'

The two women looked at each other, each lost in her own thoughts. Lauren was the first to speak.

'Then you won't be coming back to the shop even when your wrist is better.'

Daisy shook her head. 'I'm so sorry. We had such plans, didn't we? But I can't leave Morice.'

Lauren took Daisy's hands in hers. 'Of course you can't. Morice is a darling and he worships you. I'll just have to rethink my ideas.'

Jake returned to the table. 'Still looking thoughtful. What's on your mind, or is it a secret?'

'No, it's not a secret. It's Daisy.' She told him about their conversation and Daisy's news.

'Can you replace her?'

'I expect so. But it won't be the same. Daisy and I have worked together since the shop opened. I shall miss her. She's a friend, not just a colleague.'

'What about Jason?'

'Jason is moving on at Christmas. He's had another offer. Pity; he's very good.' She bit into her sandwich. 'Let's not think about it now. Tell me about Sunday. What time do we leave?'

★　★　★

On Sunday morning there was a tap at her door. Lauren was ready early in her new navy corduroy jacket and red trousers. She'd been waiting for an opportunity to wear them.

She opened the door. Jake stood there holding the hand of a fair-haired small boy. Lauren didn't need an introduction to know that this was Alfi.

'Your shoes are like the Wicked Witch in the story,' said Alfi.

'Alfi is an avid reader,' Jake explained apologetically.

Lauren opened the door wider and they came into the flat. Alfi looked around. 'You don't have any children,' he remarked. 'No toys.'

'Er — no.' Lauren wasn't sure how to take this observant child. 'But I have some children's books. Would you like to see them?'

Alfi was soon engrossed in her small collection. 'I'm sorry about this,' Jake said softly, nodding towards his son. 'Marilyn has to go and see her mother. She's not well, and Alfi would be in the way. So I offered ...'

'Of course,' said Lauren. 'I shall love getting to know him.'

'My mother will be pleased,' said Jake. 'She doesn't get the chance to see him as often as she'd like. Come along, young man,' he called. 'Time we were off.'

'May I borrow this book?' asked Alfi. 'I can read it on the way.'

Lauren took the small, brightly coloured book he held out. '*The Tale of Peter Rabbit.* That was always one of my favourites. Of course you can borrow it.'

Alfi opened the book and settled into the corner of the back seat as they set off.

'Don't read all the way,' warned his father. 'It'll be bad for your eyes. Look at the scenery too.'

'The scenery isn't very interesting at the moment,' Alfi commented. 'When we get to the countryside, I'll put the book down.'

'How far away is your mother's house?' asked Lauren.

'About a hundred and fifty miles. We'll be there by eleven. Just in time for coffee.'

'I'm not allowed coffee,' piped a small voice from the back.

'I'm sure Granny will have something suitable for you.'

'Look,' said Lauren over her shoulder, 'sheep, cows, fields — we're in the countryside now.'

'Can we play I Spy?' asked Alfi.

Jake smiled apologetically at Lauren.

'Good idea,' she called to the small boy. 'You go first.'

The game occupied the next half hour, and they were soon on the outskirts of Langton Bay.

'Mother lives on the far side of the town. The house overlooks the sea.'

'How wonderful. I've always longed for a house overlooking the sea.' Lauren looked eagerly ahead and was soon rewarded by a glimpse of a wide stretch of calm water glittering in the midday sun.

'The sea! The sea!' shouted Alfi.

Jake turned a corner and pulled into a wide drive. Now they could see the sea properly. But before Alfi could beg to be taken down to the shore, the front door opened and Mrs. Viner stood waiting for them. Ignoring Lauren, she held out her arms to Alfi. Obediently he ran to her and was hugged.

Lauren watched the scene. There was something over the top in Mrs. Viner's greeting of her little grandson. It was as though she was making a demonstration.

At last she stood up and smiled at Jake and Lauren. It seemed a forced smile that didn't reach her eyes. Lauren could see no resemblance between Jake and his mother. Perhaps he took after his father. Mrs. Viner had the sort of hair that looked as if it would never be out of place. Her make up was perfect. She wore an expensive-looking navy skirt and a blue and white flowered blouse. Lauren wondered whether her own clothes were too casual. But it was a seaside resort, she thought defiantly. Casual is correct for that.

Jake bent and gave his mother a kiss. 'This is my friend, Lauren,' he said, bringing her forward.

Mrs. Viner held out a hand. 'Any friend of Jake's is welcome.' Lauren felt there was an emphasis on the word 'friend'.

Jake smiled encouragingly and led Lauren into the house. It was a warm day, but the house felt cold. Perhaps it was the abundance of white, thought Lauren. The walls gleamed harshly, with few pictures to soften them. In the sitting-room, the couch and armchairs were of white leather. A stark white coffee table stood in the middle of a fluffy white hearthrug. *However does she keep it all clean?* Lauren wondered. But it seemed as though Mrs. Viner was the sole occupant of the house, so perhaps it wasn't difficult.

Jake's mother came into the room carrying a tray of coffee. Lauren reached into her bag and brought out a cake box. 'I've brought you some cakes from my shop,' she said, handing the box to the other woman.

Mrs. Viner took the box and put it on a table nearby. 'Thank you,' she said, 'but I've made some cheese scones. They're nice and warm, just the way you like them.' She beamed at Jake, who looked uncomfortable.

'Lauren made the cakes herself,' he informed his mother.

'I thought she said she bought them from a shop.'

'My shop,' said Lauren. 'I've brought them from my shop.'

'So you work in a cake shop,' said Mrs. Viner.

Before Jake or Lauren could say that Lauren owned the cake shop, Alfi demanded his granny's attention in the garden.

'I'm so sorry,' Jake said. 'Mother

isn't exactly welcoming, I'm afraid. It's nothing to do with you. Marilyn is the problem. Mother thinks the world of her and blames me for the divorce.'

'But she went off with someone else, didn't she?'

'Yes. And Mother knows it, but she still blames me. It'll be difficult for anyone to take Marilyn's place, in her eyes. And of course she's seen less of Alfi, which is also my fault.'

Lauren was unsure of how to deal with Jake's mother. Should she keep quiet and try to fade into the background, or talk to the older woman, offer to help, and pretend she hadn't noticed the unfriendliness? She hadn't decided by the time they were called to lunch.

The meal was excellent. Mrs. Viner was a very good cook. Lauren complimented her and was rewarded with a thin smile.

'The recipe is one of Elvin Tate's. You know, the TV chef. I always watch his programmes. He's wonderful.'

Lauren wondered whether to

acknowledge her father and perhaps be in Mrs. Viner's good books forever. But she dismissed this idea. She wanted Jake's mother to like her for herself, not because of her father.

Lunch over, Lauren tentatively offered to dry the dishes. 'No need,' said the other woman. 'They're in the dishwasher.'

'Time to go to the beach,' said Jake cheerfully. 'Are you coming, Mother?'

'Of course. Alfi and I are going to build sandcastles. Your old bucket and spade are still in the cupboard under the stairs. We'll take them with us.'

They set off, Jake carrying a large beach mat and Alfi the bucket and spade. Lauren was allowed to carry the picnic basket containing drinks and biscuits.

As soon as his mother was settled on the beach mat and Alfi had begun his sandcastle construction, Jake put out a hand to Lauren and drew her to her feet. 'Lauren and I need a walk after that car journey,' he said. We shan't be long.'

They set off across the soft, damp sand. 'We'll walk round the bay,' he said. 'It'll really stretch our legs, and Mother can have Alfi to herself for a nice long time. I'm sorry she isn't being friendly,' he said again.

'Perhaps I shouldn't have come,' said Lauren. 'But I'm glad I did.' She gave him a smile. 'It's so lovely and fresh after days in a hot kitchen.'

'Well I'm glad you came. And I want you to come again. Mother must just get used to you and accept you.'

She looked at him curiously. 'Why?' she asked. 'Why must she get used to me?'

'Well ...' Jake looked a little uncomfortable. He put an arm round her shoulders and gave her a hug. 'Because you're my friend. Come on, there's an ice cream hut. Let's get one.'

'I expect you spent a lot of time on this beach as a child,' said Lauren as they sat on a large smooth rock and ate strawberry ice creams.

'Mm. As a child, I came here often to build sandcastles and paddle. When I was a teenager it was swimming and beach parties. We often came at night and made little fires for light, and someone would bring a guitar and we'd dance. It was great fun.'

He was silent, remembering. Lauren thought of her own childhood spent in flats above restaurants and felt envious.

Jake stood up. 'Come on, let's walk.' They walked, it seemed, for miles on the edge of splashy waves. Lauren breathed deeply. The air was so fresh and tingly. How lovely to live near the sea. Perhaps she could find a cake shop in a seaside town.

Jake glanced at his watch. 'Three o'clock. We should go back now. We'll need to leave at five to get Alfi home in time for bed.'

Lauren looked round the bay at the soft sand and pale grey rocks; at the gentle, sparkling waves and the calling seagulls. 'I want to imprint this scene on my mind so that I can imagine it when I'm roasting in a hot kitchen,' she said with a laugh. 'It'll cool me down.'

'We'll come again,' Jake promised. 'Even in winter it's lovely here, if you wrap up well.'

Mrs Viner and Alfi were eating biscuits and proudly contemplating a large elaborate sand castle when they returned. They'd worked hard. There was a moat which Alfi had despaired of filling with seawater.

'Every time I pour the water in it goes away,' he said, flinging out his arms dramatically.

The castle had turrets at each corner and a stone bridge crossing the moat. Jake and Lauren were loud in their praise. Alfi beamed as Lauren walked round it several times.

'I can see one thing that it needs,' she said, 'and I think I have it. Find a little stick.'

Alfi found an old lollipop stick in the sand. Lauren took from her handbag a small case containing paper tissues. They were printed with the union flag. Carefully she threaded the stick through the edge of a tissue.

'A flag!' shouted Alfi. 'What a good idea. Castles have to have flags.' He pressed it into the top of a turret and jumped up and down as the paper flag flapped in the breeze.

'I don't think the union flag is a suitable subject for a paper tissue,' Mrs. Viner said, frowning at the flag.

'Someone gave them to me at the Queen's Jubilee,' said Lauren. 'I don't use them.'

'I should hope not. Do you want some coffee?' Mrs. Viner took out a thermos flask and two cups.

Lauren took her cup, feeling a little deflated. She'd only made the flag to please Alfi. What would it take to please his grandmother?

* * *

Lauren arrived early at the shop next morning but Paulina and Jason were there before her. They were carefully decorating a large tray of cupcakes. Jason was swirling pink, white and chocolate buttercream onto the tops of the cakes and Paulina was sprinkling nuts, cherries

118

and tiny sweets onto the cream. They looked almost guilty when Lauren opened the door.

'I hope you don't mind,' said Jason, 'but we thought we'd make extra cupcakes today. They went so well last week.'

Lauren studied the cakes. They were so pretty, like a carpet of flowers. 'No, I don't mind at all,' she said. 'But it's extra work for you.'

'We are happy,' said Paulina. 'We enjoy it.'

Lauren made them all a cup of coffee. Did she mind? They were showing initiative, but were they also taking over? She supposed that Jason, as a chef, was used to making decisions. And Paulina would happily go along with whatever he suggested.

As Jason had predicted, the cupcakes were a great success, and they'd sold out before lunch.

'I'll make another batch this afternoon ready for decorating tomorrow,' he said.

'I think I'll put silver balls on the white ones and those tiny flowers on the pink ones,' said Paulina. She picked up a cake tray and danced around the kitchen table.

'You're very happy,' Lauren commented.

'Happy. Happy,' sang Paulina. 'Yes, I'm happy.'

Lauren looked at Jason, who coloured up and looked rather embarrassed. Whatever was going on?

When the shop was closed and they'd cleaned and scrubbed all the surfaces, Jason sat at the table and patted the seat beside him. 'Come and sit down, Lauren, and discuss an idea,' he said. Paulina sat opposite, looking avidly interested.

'It's your shop,' Jason began. 'Say no and we shan't mention our idea again, but …' He hesitated.

'Yes?' prompted Lauren. 'I can't say anything until you tell me your idea.'

Jason took a deep breath. 'White walls are fresh and clean,' he began.

Lauren looked at him curiously. 'It sounds like the first line of a poem,' she said with a nervous laugh.

'What I mean is, don't you think

pale-coloured walls, like the cream on the cupcakes, would look pretty and, well, cake-like? One could be cream and one pink. Then there's pistachio and lilac, or pale blue.'

'The colours of the cupcakes,' said Paulina with a smile.

Lauren thought. 'I agree it would look pretty and appropriate,' she said. 'But I don't know that I want the expense of decorating.'

'If you buy the paint, Ray and I will do it,' said Jason.

Paulina nodded vigorously. 'I too will help.'

After a lot more discussion, Lauren found herself agreeing, and a date was set for the decorating. As she drove home, Lauren wondered why she'd given in to two people who, only a few weeks ago, she hadn't even known.

I suppose it was because Daisy isn't here now and won't be again. Everything has changed. I feel disorientated, not in control. But that's silly. It's still my business. I am in control.

She walked up the stairs, hoping that Jake would hear her arrive and come over. But the corridor was quiet and empty and Jake's door remained firmly closed. *I shan't call on him*, she decided, *but I do wish he'd come over. I really want to talk to someone.*

7

The little bell on the back of the shop door tinkled. Lauren came out of the kitchen to see a tall, fair-haired young man studying the cupcakes in the glass-fronted counter.

'Are these what they call cupcakes?' he asked without looking up.

'Yes,' Lauren answered. *I'm sure I know you*, she thought.

He straightened up and looked at her. Recognition came to both of them at the same time.

'We met at ...' they both began.

'The operatic society,' finished Lauren. 'Have you performed your show yet?'

'Next month,' he said. 'You didn't come back.'

'No. It wasn't really me. I hope you managed to find another partner.'

He smiled. 'A very good one. In fact, we've become partners in more ways than one.'

'I'm so glad. Did you want some cup-cakes for her?'

'She's always on about them. I thought I'd give her a surprise.'

Lauren opened a cake box and the young man chose four highly decorated cakes. She took the money and handed him the box. 'I hope she enjoys them. Bye, Alan.'

He looked confused. 'Goodbye, er …'

'Lauren,' she said.

'Of course. Goodbye, Lauren.'

Lauren smiled to herself. Fancy seeing him again. The incident reminded her of her friends' intention to find her a boyfriend. Alan was Jane's contribution. Then Daisy and Morice had produced Ray.

And I've found Jake on my own, she thought. But Jake wasn't a boyfriend. He was becoming a very close friend, but still only a friend. His face came into her mind; a smiling face with bright blue eyes and curls that fell onto his forehead no matter how often he tossed them back.

Thinking of him and some of the fun times they'd had together, she leaned against the counter, lost in a happy reverie.

Jason came up behind her and made her jump. 'The meringues are ready,' he said. 'D'you want to fill them, or should Paulina?'

Recalled to the present, Lauren followed him into the kitchen. 'I'll do the meringues,' she said to Paulina. 'You finish the cream slices and put them on to that tray.' No time to think of Jake or any other man. Her business must come first.

★   ★   ★

Her father telephoned just as she was leaving the shop. 'Can you come for dinner? I want to talk about something.'

'Is it important? OK, but I can't stay late.'

He was waiting for her when she arrived at La Belle Étoile. 'I'm glad you've come early,' he said. 'We're almost empty until eight o'clock, so we can talk.'

'What's wrong?' asked Lauren. 'Has something happened?'

'Dinner first. Serious conversation spoils good food.'

They ate superb slow-roasted lamb followed by a raspberry tart with thick golden clotted cream. Lauren agreed with her father that conversation would have spoiled the food.

But when coffee and mints had been served, he said suddenly, 'Petros wants to leave La Belle Fleur.'

She was startled. 'Petros! But he *is* La Belle Fleur. People come from miles to eat there just because of him.'

'D'you think I don't know it?' Her father's face was a mask of misery. 'Where am I going to find a replacement for him?'

They were silent, thinking. Then her father gave her a sideways look. 'Unless, of course, you would consider ...'

'Let's not have that argument again,' she said. 'You'll have to ask around and do some head-hunting.' As she spoke, Jason's name flashed into her mind. She didn't know how good a chef he was

— she'd have to speak to Ray — but she'd bear him in mind.

★　★　★

A few days later, Daisy turned up at the shop. Her arm was out of its plaster, and she looked bright and very smart in a fuchsia suit and matching shoes.

'There's nothing wrong with you now,' said Lauren. 'Have you come back to work?'

Daisy laughed. 'I can give you an hour or two if you like, but I'm very busy at the moment.'

'Is your arm better? Are you driving?'

'Yes it's much better, and no I'm not driving. I came by taxi. I've brought you a surprise.' She fumbled in her bag, brought out a card embossed with gold writing, and handed it to Lauren.

'Daisy! You're getting married!'

'And that's your invitation.' They fell into each other's arms.

'Oh Daisy, I'm so pleased.' Tears welled up in Lauren's eyes.

'Well don't cry about it. You're supposed to be happy for me.'

'Oh I am, I am. And for Morice. He's a lucky man.'

'It's not a church wedding, I'm afraid. There wasn't time to arrange that.'

'Wasn't time? You mean …?'

'Yes. We're off to America in three weeks. Morice signed the contract for a year with an option for two more. So we decided to get married, sell up and move to America. The band is coming with us, of course, except for Ray.'

Lauren looked at her questioningly.

'He wouldn't leave Jason without a flatmate.'

Lauren looked at her friend. They'd shared so many dreams and ideas. She'd never imagined that Daisy would leave her. 'Three years,' she said. 'I'll miss you dreadfully.'

'As soon as we're settled, you must come over. America is no distance away now.' She stood up. 'I'll see you at the registry office, then. Don't be late.' She glanced at her watch. 'I told the taxi to be back in half an hour.' She peeped out of the window. 'There he is.' She gave Lauren a kiss. 'Bye. See you.' And she was gone.

Lauren watched her friend climb into the taxi. This was a new self-assured Daisy, ready for a new life in a new country.

Jason and Paulina were chattering in the kitchen. *Time for me to make plans with different people*, Lauren thought. She couldn't rely on Daisy anymore. She went into the kitchen.

'We're going to try out the biscuits next week,' she said. 'I have all the equipment here. Jason, if you could make up some of these shapes, I'll see what I can do with Daisy's exotic food colours. She bought silver and gold, so we should be able to glamorise the biscuits.'

Jason glanced at Paulina, who looked down at the ground. 'Go on,' he urged. 'Show her.'

Paulina quivered excitedly but didn't move.

'Go on,' said Jason in a firmer tone.

Lauren looked from one to the other.

129

'Paulina has something to show you,' said Jason.

The young woman went to a cupboard on the wall and took out a box. She opened it and handed it to Lauren. Inside was a pile of papers cut into the shapes of biscuits. Each one was exquisitely decorated in vibrant colours. Some had a Christmas theme — a fairy, a stocking, a Christmas tree; some had just a glowing panel of colours like a stained-glass window.

Lauren looked from the pictures to Paulina. 'You did these?'

Paulina nodded.

'But they're beautiful. Why didn't you say you could design like this?'

'Nobody asked me.'

'Well,' Lauren said, subsiding into the nearest chair. 'Paulina, would you be happy to decorate the new biscuits? I could never do them so beautifully.'

Paulina clapped her hands together. 'I would be happy. I would be so happy.'

Lauren and Jason smiled at each other. 'So our project can go ahead,' said

Lauren. 'Daisy ordered some very smart boxes, so we can start our new line at once. It'll mean a lot of extra work, but I'm sure it'll be worth it.'

★   ★   ★

Daisy's wedding day was fine but cold. Lauren was glad she had a nearly new cream wool coat which went well over the new jade-coloured dress she'd bought on her shopping day with Daisy. She had also bought a little cream fur pillbox hat which Paulina assured her looked very glamorous.

Ray, smart in a dark suit, picked Lauren up and drove her to the registry office. There was a coolness in his greeting to Jason and Paulina which puzzled her, but there was no time to wonder about it.

It was a small wedding group, mostly Daisy's relations and the band. Morice's family lived in Barbados, too far to travel.

Daisy looked beautiful in a white fitted dress and a white fur jacket. Her face lit up when she saw Lauren. Lauren and Ray were the last to arrive, and when they were seated the ceremony began.

Daisy had often talked about her dreams of getting married in church. She would sweep down the aisle in a flowing white dress, 'like an angel', as she put it.

Lauren looked at Daisy's face and at Morice as they made their vows. *The setting doesn't matter*, she thought. *Church or registry office, it's the words and the feelings that count.*

Morice looked at Daisy with all the love in the world on his face. *I wonder if someone will look at me like that one day*, Lauren thought.

The registrar pronounced them husband and wife. Morice took Daisy in his arms and the guests broke into wild applause.

Lauren drove to the reception with Ray. He was very quiet.

'What will you do when they've gone to America?' she asked him. 'Can you find another band?'

He gave a shuddering sigh. 'I haven't

belonged to this one very long. But yes, I'll have to put out some feelers.'

'You wouldn't go with them?' she asked tentatively.

'I can't leave Jason. He needs me.'

Lauren thought of the little scene in the kitchen and wondered.

They'd reached the hotel where the reception was to be held. Inside, they were conducted to a small circular room in the centre of which was a large round table.

'We're all sitting together,' Morice announced. 'There aren't enough of us for individual tables, and this is friendlier.'

Though the bride and groom were leaving friends and family for three years, perhaps even longer, it was a happy meal with lots of laughter.

Across the table, Daisy blew Lauren a kiss. *You next*, she mouthed.

Lauren shook her head. Marriage definitely didn't feature in her future plans.

★　★　★

When she returned to the shop, Jason and Paulina were clearing up. She heard their laughter as she opened the shop door. Obviously they hadn't missed her.

Ray came in with her. 'I'll give you a lift home when you're ready,' he said to Jason.

Lauren caught the look of disappointment on Paulina's face. What was going on? When Ray and Jason had left together Lauren sat at the table and indicated that Paulina should sit too.

'Paulina,' she began, 'this is difficult, but I must talk to you.'

The Polish woman looked at her expectantly.

'About Jason,' Lauren began. 'You're very friendly. You work well together.'

Paulina blushed. 'I love him,' she said.

'Oh dear,' said Lauren. 'Paulina, you're very young. I feel responsible for you as you're working for me. Don't get too involved with Jason until you know him better.'

'And he loves me,' said Paulina.

'Oh dear,' said Lauren again. She felt

out of her depth, unsure what to say next.

Paulina stood up. 'I'm sorry, I have to go. My friend Anya is calling for me this evening. We are going to a new club. I have to change. I will see you in the morning early.'

She was gone, leaving Lauren sitting at the table wondering what to do. Poor Ray. It looked as if he was going to have another change to his life soon.

★ ★ ★

'I'm going to visit my mother tomorrow,' said Jake. 'She has various little jobs she'd like some help with. Would you like to come? A day at the seaside would do you good.'

But will a day with your mother? thought Lauren.

He seemed to sense her doubt. 'Look, I know my mother can be ... well, difficult, but she has reason. As I explained, she thinks a lot of Marilyn, and anyone else ...'

'But your divorce was nothing to do

135

with me,' Lauren protested. 'We didn't know each other then.'

Jake looked downcast. 'So you'd rather not come.'

'Of course I'll come, if you want me to.'

He brightened up. 'Once you get to know each other, she'll be different,' he said with what Lauren felt wasn't great conviction.

But how could she turn down a day with him? She'd so enjoyed the last time. They wouldn't spend all day with his mother. There might be time for a walk alone on the beach.

'I can't come early,' she said. 'I've got someone coming to see me at nine. I'm sorry. You won't want to leave as late as ten, will you?'

'Ten will be fine,' he said. 'As long as you're coming with me.'

She felt he deserved an explanation. 'A friend of Margaret's at the food college phoned to ask if she could bring some large cakes to show me. She's lost her usual outlet and passed my shop one day and wondered whether we could do business.'

'Does she make them at home?'

'Yes. Why?'

'What about hygiene and so on?'

'I'll ask to see her certificates, of course. If she's satisfactory, it might be a big help to have someone making some of the stock. Jason won't be with me after Christmas, so I'll have a problem again until I get someone in his place.'

Jake stood up and stretched his arms above his head. 'I must go. I've got some papers to look at before bed. I'll be over for you at ten.'

* * *

Margaret's friend knocked on Lauren's door at the stroke of nine. She carried four cake boxes tied one on top of the other in each hand. She introduced herself as Denise Black. Lauren helped her in with the boxes and invited her to take off her coat and scarf.

'I've got some coffee ready,' she said. 'We can drink as we talk.'

Denise placed the boxes carefully on the table and unfastened each one. Lauren was impressed as each cake was revealed but said nothing until Denise had unfastened the last one.

'They look most impressive,' she said at last. 'Oh, you've put labels on each one.'

'Yes. Coffee, chocolate, carrot, strawberry,' Denise read out the labels proudly. Each cake was beautifully decorated with buttercream icing, artificial fruits and flowers, and silver balls. Lauren could imagine they'd make an inviting display in the shop window. Some looked like glamorous hats and one resembled a jewelled crown.

Denise took another smaller box from her capacious shoulder bag. 'I've brought some samples for you to try,' she said, and opened the box to reveal eight small cakes.

Lauren smiled with pleasure. 'I'll try them with my coffee. I haven't had much breakfast.'

They ate the cakes between them and chatted about the recipes. 'I don't often make large cakes, except to order,' said Lauren. 'It'll be interesting to see how these sell.'

Denise looked pleased. 'Then you'd like to …'

'Oh yes. I definitely want to try them.'

Denise reached into her bag again. 'I've got my hygiene certificates here.' She handed them to Lauren. They discussed the business side of the transaction, and it was ten to ten before Denise stood up to go.

'I'm sure we'll work very well together,' said Lauren. They smiled at each other.

'I'll see you at the shop at eight on Tuesday,' said Denise.

As she closed the door, Lauren glanced at the clock. Ten minutes! She'd eaten her lipstick with the cake. She dashed into her bedroom to repair the damage, put on her outdoor shoes and grab her coat.

She was fastening the last button when Jake rang the doorbell.

★   ★   ★

Mrs. Viner's welcome was scarcely warmer than the last time.

'Lauren came with me to keep me company on the journey,' said Jake with a little laugh.

That sounds like an apology for bringing me, thought Lauren. She handed a little posy of flowers to the older woman.

'How very kind,' said Mrs. Viner.

'Jake told me they were your favourites.'

'Yes.' Mrs. Viner buried her nose in the freesias. 'Marilyn always brings these when she comes to see me. I'll find a vase for them.'

Lauren gave Jake a rueful smile. She'd tried her best. She could do no more.

Jake stood up. 'Come along, Mother. Get your coat. We're taking you out for lunch.'

'Oh no.' Mrs. Viner sat down. 'That's not necessary. I can do something here.'

'I said we're going out for lunch.' Jake helped Lauren with her coat. 'Are you coming or shall we see you later?'

'Very well,' said his mother ungraciously. 'I'll get my coat.'

Thank goodness, thought Lauren. It would be easier to cope with Jake's mother in a noisy, impersonal restaurant than in the claustrophobic atmosphere of the house.

Surprisingly, Lauren found herself enjoying the meal. Jake put himself out to be amusing, and his mother, on her best behaviour in public, smiled and joined in the chatter.

They returned to the house. Mrs. Viner wanted help with hanging some curtains in her bedroom. With Lauren's assistance, Jake was able to complete the job and replace some batteries in various pieces of equipment.

Mrs. Viner was so pleased that she began to talk to Lauren in a friendly fashion, and after tea and cake they were able to leave without any more animosity.

'She's getting better, I think,' said Jake. 'She just needs time to get used to you.'

Do I really want to be put through this? Lauren asked herself. *Is friendship with Jake worth this aggravation?*

Jake glanced across at her as if reading

her thoughts. 'Thanks for coming with me,' he said. He gave her one of his melting smiles, took her hand in his, and gave it a squeeze.

Lauren wrapped her fingers around his. *Yes*, she thought. *It's worth it.*

8

Paulina and Jason's decorating day soon came round. Ray had been deputed to get the paint and arrived with a large tin of rose pink, another of mint green, one of lavender, and another of cream. The furniture and counter were to be of shining white.

Lauren called in to make sure they had all they needed, though they made it quite plain they didn't want her to stay.

'We want you to have a surprise on Monday morning,' said Paulina. 'A nice surprise, I hope.'

'Make a start while I cook some bacon butties for you,' said Lauren. 'They'll keep you going.'

While she was cooking, Ray came into the kitchen. He closed the door quietly behind him. 'I had a word with Jason about La Belle Fleur,' he said. 'I thought he'd jump at the chance, but he said he had other plans. I don't understand. I know he's been offered another position, but only at an ordinary restaurant, nothing like La Belle Fleur.'

'Did he tell you what his other plans were?' Lauren cut the thick bacon sandwiches and placed them on three plates.

'No. He wouldn't say. We never keep things from each other. Why wouldn't he tell me?' Misery was stamped all over his face. Lauren was sure that Jason's plans concerned Paulina, and she began to wish the woman had never come to the shop. Ray was her friend and she hated to see him so unhappy.

'I expect he wants it to be a surprise for you,' she said cheerfully. 'Don't worry about it; he's just being mysterious.'

Ray brightened up a little. 'Perhaps you're right. Shall I call the others if you're ready?'

'I know you want to get rid of me,' she said to Jason and Paulina as they attacked their sandwiches, 'but I can't stay anyway. I'm going to see a friend to discuss a plan for the shop.'

'You've found another partner?' asked Jason, and Lauren detected a note of disappointment in his voice.

'No. Margaret is a lecturer at the College of Food and not interested in a cake shop. My idea is to take some of her students — perhaps two at a time — and give them the experience of working in a retail food environment. They could come perhaps twice a week. We shouldn't need to pay them, and we'd have some extra help. What do you think?'

Paulina didn't look very enthusiastic. *Perhaps she sees young female students as rivals*, thought Lauren. But Jason considered the suggestion.

'It could be a good idea,' he said. 'Have we room for two more staff?'

'I'd thought of having one of the storerooms converted into an extra kitchen. It'd be useful in so many ways.'

Jason crammed the last piece of bacon sandwich into his mouth and stood up. 'I'm in favour of it,' he said. 'Go and see your friend and tell us what you've decided tomorrow. Now, come on you lazy decorators. To work!'

* * *

Margaret was a typical no-nonsense sort of college tutor, tall and dark-haired with a face that looked severe in repose but lit up when she smiled. She and Lauren had become firm friends when they had both studied at the College of Food.

'I put the coffee on when I saw you coming through the park gates,' Margaret said. 'It's ready now.'

'I've brought you some of my new mince pies.' Lauren handed over a box. 'They're my latest creation.'

The pies were tasted and approved. For a while the two sat and chatted idly. Then Margaret asked, 'Heard from Steve lately?'

'Not lately, not ever,' said Lauren. 'Steve is history.'

Margaret took another pie. 'So who's present-day?'

'No one. I'm heart-free.'

'I find that hard to believe.'

'I have a friend,' Lauren said. 'I repeat, friend. We go out together as friends. Neither of us wants anything more.' She spoke decidedly but felt a frisson of doubt. He might want nothing more, but did she?

Margaret smiled. It was a 'we'll see' sort of smile. But she made no comment.

'Shall we discuss my idea for the students?' Lauren was anxious to change the subject.

'I've spoken to the principal,' said her friend. 'She's very keen on the idea. But it must be voluntary. No forced labour.'

'Of course,' agreed Lauren. 'We can only take one or two at a time — you know the size of the shop — and there are three of us working there already.'

'Who are the other two? You've lost Daisy, haven't you? Will she come back?'

'She's married and living in America now. She won't be back. I've had to re-arrange my plans.' She told Margaret about Jason and Paulina. 'They're both very good, but somehow I feel unsettled without Daisy.'

Margaret nodded sympathetically. 'I expect it'll all work out in the end. Now, I have a favour to ask.'

'Ask away.'

'Do you think you could persuade your father to give out the prizes at the end of the Christmas term?'

'How close to Christinas will it be? He's very busy just then, as you can imagine.'

'About ten days before. We'd be so grateful.'

'I'll see what I can do.' Lauren stood up. 'Shall we say two students in one week's time?'

'I'll phone to confirm it.' Margaret saw her off at the door. Lauren crossed the road towards the park.

I wonder how the decorators are getting on. She breathed deeply. It was lovely to be out in the fresh air after days spent in a steamy kitchen. *That reminds me, I must get some quotes for the conversion of the storeroom.*

At the gate to the park she stopped and consulted her watch. Should she go home or go shopping? She reached into her coat pocket and pulled out a coin. Heads home, tails shopping, she decided. She threw the coin into the air.

'Boo,' said a voice behind her.

The coin missed her hand and fell on the ground. Jake's foot covered it.

'Let me see it,' she said. 'I'm making a decision.'

'About what?'

'Whether to go home or shopping.'

'Which is home, heads or tails?'

'Heads,' said Lauren.

Jake moved his foot and picked up the coin before she could see it. 'Heads,' he said. 'Come on. Home.'

'Why?'

'Because we're going out. You promised to go for a walk with me. This is an ideal day. We're both free.' He took her arm and hurried her in the direction of the flats.

'Since you're being all masterful,' she said, 'where have you decided we're going?'

'Pennet Hill. There's a nice little pub

at the top. We can have lunch there then go for a ramble.'

Half an hour later they set off. Lauren wore a warm hooded jacket and comfortable shoes. The sky, which had been bright and autumnal in the morning, had begun to cloud over.

'What if it rains?' she asked as she climbed into Jake's car.

'It won't rain,' he said airily. 'Look, there's even a bit of sunshine.'

'Very watery sun,' she answered. 'The afternoon's not as nice as this morning.'

Jake parked at the bottom of Pennet Hill and they began the climb up the steep road to the top. They could see the little pub, but even after half an hour of walking it still seemed as far away as ever.

'Let's have a rest,' Lauren gasped, leaning on a gate and looking across the fields. 'Isn't it peaceful? No one here except us.'

'And no rain,' said Jake.

'That's tempting fate. Let's go on. I'm hungry, and goodness knows how long it'll take us to get there.'

The Pennet Inn was small and squat

with thick walls to keep out the hilltop winds. Tempting smells of roasting food wafted through the front door as they entered.

'At last,' gasped Lauren. 'I thought we'd never get here.'

The room was quite full, but most of their fellow diners had come by car. Lauren felt that she and Jake deserved a meal more than the others after their steep climb. Eagerly she scanned the menu.

Before long, they were tucking into steak and kidney pies. Jake grinned at her across the table. 'You have a shiny nose.'

'You're not immaculate yourself,' she retorted, flushing under his gaze.

'You look beautiful when you're angry,' he said.

'How original. Eat your pie.'

'I've finished.' He replaced his knife and fork. 'Drinks. What would you like?'

Lauren watched his tall figure make its way through the crowd to the bar. Dear Jake. He was such good company; cheerful, relaxed, handsome. What more could a woman desire? But he was not available, not in the market. He enjoyed his life as it was. He had no need of a girlfriend.

She sighed. She fancied him, there was no denying it. Whatever she said to her friends, she knew that if the right man came along, she would fall. And Jake was the right man.

'You look miles away.' He was putting two long glasses on the table. 'Lager, will that do?'

She was thirsty and the lager was just right. 'Where shall we walk?' she asked. 'Do you know the area?'

'Not really. We'll just wander.'

The road to the Pennet Inn carried on further up the hill. 'Let's walk to the top,' he said. 'It's not much further on, and the views will be spectacular.'

They set off. Before they reached the top, Lauren felt a few spots of rain. She looked at Jake. 'There's no shelter up here. We'll get soaked if it rains heavily.'

Jake looked up at the darkening sky. 'Mm. We'll leave the top for another time.

Let's get back to the inn.'

When they returned to the inn, Jake said, 'Go inside and wait. I'll get down to the car faster without you, then I can come back for you. No point in both of us getting soaked.'

'No, I'm coming with you. Let's go.'

They hurried down the road. By now it had begun to rain in earnest. Lauren's coat was warm and waterproof, but it was unable to keep out the relentless downpour.

'Lauren, I'm sorry. This walk wasn't a good idea, was it?'

'It wasn't raining when we set out. Don't worry about it. We've nearly reached the car.'

They sat uncomfortably in their wet clothes as Jake drove quickly home. Lauren began to sneeze.

Jake glanced at her anxiously. 'Get your wet clothes off and get into a hot shower as soon as you can. This is the second time I've driven you home soaking wet. I hope there won't be a third.'

'We'd better not go out in a boat,' she

said between shivers.

Sitting by the fire in a warm towelling robe, her hair wrapped in a towel, Lauren thought back over the day. It had started so happily. Now Jake would have a feeling of guilt and perhaps not suggest another trip.

There was a tap at the door. Jake came in holding a lemon, a jar of honey and a bottle of whisky. 'Just in case you haven't got them,' he said, indicating the things in his hands, 'I've come to make you a hot toddy.'

'That's very kind. Make one for yourself too.' She went back to her seat by the fire and sneezed again.

Jake disappeared into the kitchen and was soon back with two steaming mugs. He handed her one and took the seat opposite, close to the fire. 'Drink it up and get into bed,' he said. 'You'll probably feel better by the morning.'

★   ★   ★

But Lauren didn't feel better. She took her temperature and groaned at the result. She felt shivery and her throat was tight. There was no way she could go to the shop.

As soon as she was sure someone would be there, she phoned. Jason answered. She explained the situation.

'Don't worry,' he said brightly. 'We'll manage. Just get better.'

Lauren crawled back to bed. When Jake called to see her, she buried her face in the pillow. 'Don't look at me, I look like a beetroot,' she groaned. 'Go away.'

' Can I get you anything to eat?'

'No, I don't want any food, only drinks, and I've got plenty of those. I'll see you next week.'

Jake laughed. 'I think I'll see you before that. You've got my number. Phone if you need me.'

I won't phone. I'll be ill on my own in peace, she thought.

He left her alone for that day, but the next evening he appeared carrying a small casserole. 'Chicken soup. Jewish grandmothers swear by it for illness.'

'What do you know about Jewish grandmothers?'

'Thank you very much.'

She eyed the casserole. Could she manage a bowl of soup?

'I shan't stay. Can't afford to catch your cold. Big deal coming up at work. I shan't see you for two days, so look after yourself, and I'll be here as soon as I get back.'

When he'd gone, Lauren tasted the soup. It was delicious. Fancy Jake being able to make something like this. She divided the soup into two bowls, one for the next day, and settled in to enjoy it.

Jason and Paulina kept in touch with her by phone. They were doing well in the shop and had even found time to make a hundred biscuits.

'Paulina is going to start decorating this afternoon,' Jason said. 'She's a wonder. You mustn't let her go.'

I wish I could keep both of you, she thought. But Jason would be off to his new position after Christmas and she would be left with the problem of getting a replacement.

Two days later she felt much better. Jake hadn't called, so she decided to return his casserole and thank him. She knocked at his door. It was opened by a pretty young woman with blazing purple curls.

'Um …' Lauren was tongue-tied for a moment. Then she thrust the casserole at the woman. 'I'm just returning this.'

The woman took the dish. 'Jake's away at the moment. Would you like —'

Lauren turned away. 'I'm sorry, I have to go. I just came to return the dish.' She hurried back to her own flat, closed the door and leaned against it.

Jake was still away, so who was the woman? She was obviously living there. Why hadn't Jake mentioned her? So much for him not wanting a new relationship. No wonder he only wanted to be friends.

Lauren made herself a hot honey and lemon drink and sat by the fire, pulling her woollen jacket closely around her. How could she be friends with a man who had another woman living with him?

Oh Jake. I was ready to love you. I do love you, but what's the use? Once again, I love someone who doesn't love me.

She lay back in her chair for a long time, watching the artificial flames of the fire and feeling thoroughly miserable. Then a feeling of self-disgust flooded through her. What was she doing, sitting here and wallowing in misery? She still had a business to run.

She stood up and looked at her reflection in the mirror. What a pathetic sight. Lipstick would help; make her look less grey. She applied some makeup and brushed her hair. Tomorrow she would go to the shop and take up the reins again. Jason and Paulina must feel they owned the business.

She was startled by a knock at the door. Her stomach tightened. Jake! What would she say to him? Another knock. She would have to open it.

Ray stood there. 'May I come in? Jason said you were feeling a bit better.' He handed her a bunch of cream and gold chrysanthemums.

'Ray. Thank you. I love the cream ones. Come in. I'll make us a coffee.'

Thankful she'd tidied herself up, she went into the kitchen to put the kettle on and find a flower vase. When she returned, Ray was sitting in an armchair looking thoughtful.

'Well?' Lauren placed the vase on the top of a bookcase. 'You look as if you have something on your mind. Want to share it?'

'I was lying awake all night trying to make a decision,' Ray said. 'Now I've come to put you in the picture.'

'This sounds serious.' She took a seat opposite him.

'When the band went to America, I stayed here because of Jason. We'd enjoyed sharing a flat. I didn't want to leave him in the lurch. But now …' He stopped.

'Now?' prompted Lauren.

'Now he and Paulina are partners. They want to share the flat. I'm in the way.' He took a deep breath. 'So I've made a decision. I'm going to America.'

'To America?'

'Yes. I'm going to join Morice and the band. He's been asking me to join them for weeks. They're doing well. It's a big opportunity for me. He wants Lily too — that's my wife. I'm going to contact her today.'

The kettle whistled. Lauren went into the kitchen. Rattling mugs and the coffee jar, she thought about Ray's news. She wasn't really surprised. Jason and Paulina had become very close recently.

'America will be a great chance for you. It's the place all musicians want to be, isn't it?'

Ray drank his coffee. 'I'll miss you, Lauren. You're my only real friend here.'

'We'll write,' she said. 'And I've promised Daisy to visit when they're settled, so we'll see each other then. When are you leaving?'

'On Saturday. I wanted to go as soon as I'd made up my mind.' He stood up. 'So I won't see you again until we meet in the U.S. of A.' He wrapped his arms round her and gave her a hug.

She closed the door behind him. Time

to sort her clothes for work tomorrow. She'd make an extra-early start in the morning.

The telephone rang. 'Lauren,' came Jake's voice, 'I'll be back about seven this evening. I'll see you then.'

'I'm sorry, Jake, but I'm busy this evening.' She carefully replaced the phone.

It rang again. 'Well when can I see you?'

'Jake, I don't go out with other women's men, not even as a friend. I'll see you around.'

Again she replaced the handset. Her eyes filled with tears. Jake had become a close friend. But it wouldn't work. If he now had a girlfriend, it would be the end of their friendship.

Fifteen minutes later, there was a soft tap at the door. Lauren ignored it. It came again. She flung open the door.

It was the woman from Jake's flat. 'Please, may I come in for a moment? We can't talk here.'

Lauren hesitated, then opened the door

161

wider. The woman came in. She was very pretty, Lauren had to admit, even with the unnaturally vivid purple hair.

'I must explain.' Her voice was slightly breathless, as if she was nervous and wanted to get her words out quickly. 'Jake asked me to see you. He's not my boyfriend, he's my brother.'

Lauren sat down on the nearest chair. 'Your brother?'

'Yes. I'm doing a short course at the college and I'm staying with him for a few days.'

'But why didn't he say anything?'

'I rushed him, I'm afraid. I arrived the night he went away. I was supposed to be staying with a friend, but she couldn't have me at the last moment. He wasn't expecting me.'

Lauren began to laugh. 'Poor Jake. I was very cross with him.'

'So he said.' The woman joined in the laughter. 'By the way, my name is Christa.'

'You know my name.'

'I know quite a bit about you. Jake is

always talking about you.'

'Really?' Lauren was surprised. 'We're only friends.'

'He's quite smitten.'

'Oh, I don't think so. Ours is a very platonic friendship.'

'That's not the impression I got. He was very down when Marilyn went off with her old flame. You seem to have filled the space nicely.' Christa stood up. 'I must go. Work for college. We must meet up for a chat soon.'

'What are you studying?' asked Lauren as she walked her visitor to the door.

'Hairdressing and beauty. It's great.'

That explains the hair, thought Lauren. *It makes her look quite different from Jake.* She smiled to herself as she tried to imagine Jake with purple curls.

The phone rang. 'Well, can I see you?'

'Jake, I'm sorry. I jumped to the wrong conclusion.' She suddenly felt shy, thinking of Christa's remark that he was 'quite smitten'.

'I'll pick you up for dinner at eight to-morrow. I'm sure you've got your appetite back. If you haven't, I'll order chicken soup.' He replaced the phone without waiting for her reply.

9

An early-morning shaft of sunshine lit up the shop. *It's like a dish of ice cream*, thought Lauren. Walls of soft mint green and lavender, rich clotted cream and pale strawberry pink were appliquéd with huge stylised daisies. The shelves and counter were icing-sugar white.

Lauren stood in the doorway drinking in the luscious effect. Jason came out of the kitchen. 'D'you like it?'

'Like it? It's beautiful. You must have all worked so hard.'

'Well you know what they say about many hands. Let me take your bags. You're loaded.' He carried Lauren's bags and boxes into the kitchen.

'I've brought the biscuit boxes,' Lauren said. 'We have to make them up.'

'Wait till you see Paulina's designs,' said Jason. Lauren thought there was an air of proprietorial pride about him. She remembered what Ray had said about Jason and Paulina being partners now.

'Ray came to see me,' she said, not looking at him.

'So you know.'

Lauren nodded.

'I feel dreadful about it, but these things happen.'

'Ray will get over it.' She began to unpack the biscuit boxes. 'In a new country he'll probably make new friends.'

Jason didn't reply, but picked up one of the boxes and began to assemble it. 'I like these,' he said. 'White and gold. Very elegant.'

'Jason, have you been coming in as early as this every morning?' Lauren asked.

'There's a lot to do. Chefs are used to early starts, as you know.' He put down the boxes, placed trays of cakes on the table, and began to decorate them and add cream.

'Are you enjoying it as much as being in a restaurant kitchen?'

Jason was thoughtful for a moment. 'At first I thought I wouldn't,' he said, 'but now I love it. It's different, but good. A more complete job somehow.'

'And there's Paulina,' Lauren said softly.

'And there's Paulina,' he repeated 'She's the icing on the cake.'

They grinned at each other. Lauren removed her coat, put on an apron, scrubbed her hands and prepared to help Jason. 'You haven't forgotten that today the students come?' she said. 'We'll be extra busy. Perhaps Paulina had better forget about biscuits today.'

'I haven't forgotten.' Jason packed a box of butter into the fridge. 'But they're not doing a whole day at first, are they?'

'No, but we'll have to supervise them carefully. Now then, have we decided what they'll do today?'

Jason produced a piece of paper. 'I've made a few notes,' he said. 'A few suggestions. See what you think.'

Paulina came in from the shop. 'The students have arrived. What shall I do with them?'

'Show them where to put their coats,'

Lauren said. 'Find them some aprons and caps and bring them in here.' She was studying Jason's list. 'I don't think I can improve on this. You seem to have covered everything. Well done, Jason.'

'Perhaps you could show them around, Paulina. Let them see where we keep everything.'

The students, Colin and Natalie, were shy at first but soon settled down. They were obviously excited to be in the world of work rather than college. Natalie was small and dark, with bobbing curly hair and a button nose. Lauren thought she looked like a pixie. Colin was fair and thin and very tall. Useful for reaching objects on high shelves, thought Lauren.

'What do we do first?' asked Natalie, her eyes shining with anticipation.

Colin was examining the rows of jars of cake decorations on the shelves. 'Where d'you get such a fantastic range of decorations?' he asked.

'From many places — America, Italy, even Australia,' Lauren answered. 'We have catalogues and order them.'

'Look at these dear little chicks and rabbits.' Natalie pointed to two see-through containers.

'Those are for Easter cupcakes,' said Lauren. 'We have butterflies and straw-berries for the summer, little chocolates, tiny birthday-cake candles, coffee beans, Halloween decorations. Things for all the year round. I'll let you loose with those when you've been here a while,' she promised Colin, seeing his interest.

Lauren was pleased to see that they took their share of the more unpleasant jobs — scrubbing tables and mopping floors — without complaint or sullen faces. 'Tomorrow you can be more cre-ative,' she promised. 'We'll see what your cake-making skills are like.'

While Paulina took the students off to the storeroom, Lauren returned to helping Jason. They worked in silence. Lauren scooped up some buttercream and placed it in the centre of a cupcake. Then with the ease born of long practice, she worked it to the edge of the cake using small strokes of the palette knife. She reached for a tiny red rose and placed it in the centre of the cake before the icing could set.

The work was soothing. It gave her time to think of the evening before. She had wondered how Jake would greet her; whether there would be any awkwardness between them. What would Christa have said to him? How would she herself greet him?

* * *

She need not have worried. Jake behaved as he had always done. He gave her a brief kiss on the forehead, nodded approvingly that she was ready, and shepherded her down the stairs to his car.

'Where are we going?' she asked.

'Not far. It's a surprise, but I hope a nice one.'

He'd told her to wear something a bit dressy; a long skirt perhaps. She thought they must be going to a hotel. She'd put on a long velvet skirt, old but one of her favourites. The background was deep green but the pattern suggested small stained-glass windows. Her silver-grey silk top was cut high at the front but had a deep scoop at the back. She wore no bracelets, as the sleeves were long and tight, but she searched in her jewellery box for her silver drop earrings.

They drove through country lanes for about half an hour and turned into the courtyard of a large old house silhouetted against the darkening sky. Candles gleamed in every window, and as they climbed from the car a man in Tudor costume came towards them carrying a lantern.

'Good evening, my lord, my lady. Will you please follow me?' He led the way through a stone archway into another courtyard.

Lauren gave Jake an excited but puzzled look. He took her arm and they joined a crowd of people making their noisy way into the house.

'I think you're dressed just right for this evening,' Jake murmured. 'You look lovely.'

They passed through several

wood-panelled passages and came out at last into a large hall decorated with holly and other green boughs. There were rows of tables down the length of the hall, each laid with platters and goblets. Jake led her to two seats near the top of the table.

'There'll be entertainment, so we'll want a good view,' he said.

'What is this place?' she asked.

'It's called Whittington Court. It's a Tudor mansion famous for its priest holes.'

'Priest holes?'

'When it was dangerous to be a Catholic family in Tudor times, small secret rooms were built into the house to hide a priest if soldiers arrived to search the place.'

'How exciting. Can we see them?'

'Not tonight. I'll bring you again in the daytime when you can do a tour of the house.'

Suddenly, the musicians in the gallery at the end of the hall struck up a stately tune and a procession arrived: a richly dressed lord and lady and several attendants. They took their places at the head of the table, looking down the hall at their guests.

Maidservants in dull pink dresses and aprons carried in large trays piled with warm, damp cloths. 'For your hands, my lady,' said a maid. 'You eat mostly with your hands, and they get rather greasy.'

Next, manservants brought in large flagons of wine and filled the goblets in front of each visitor. Lauren took a sip, her eyes sparkling as she smiled at Jake over the rim of her goblet. This was going to be an exciting evening.

Then her attention was caught by the next group of serving maids. 'Little rolls, I think,' she said. The maids carried large round baskets of small bread rolls. Lauren placed hers on her wooden platter.

'I suppose all the food goes on here,' she said. 'It's nice and large.'

They were served generous pieces of chicken decorated with cherries. 'Her Majesty, our Good Queen Bess, loves chicken with cherries,' they were told.

Bowls of salad and vegetables were

placed in front of them, dressed with oil and lemon juice. Lauren tried to use her knife — there was no fork — on the chicken, but soon gave up and used her hands like everyone else. It was great fun.

'I'm so glad you thought of this evening,' she said to Jake. 'I've never been to anything like this before.'

He smiled, pleased at her enjoyment. 'You've got grease on the end of your nose,' he said. 'Use your cloth.'

'I don't care,' said Lauren. 'This is a fantastic meal. Did they have puddings in Tudor times, I wonder?'

'I expect people had a sweet tooth even then,' he replied. 'Ah, here we are.'

Two maids carrying trays appeared in front of them, and they were served with dishes bearing a small cream pudding in the shape of a Tudor rose.

'Thank goodness we have spoons,' Lauren said. 'I don't think I could manage this with my hands.'

'Marchpane, my lady?' asked one of the maids, and they were handed small sweets in the shape of flowers and leaves.

Lauren bit into one. 'Why, it's marzipan. What did she call it? March pane?'

Their goblets were refilled. 'Non-alcoholic,' said the manservant with a smile. 'We have to think of drivers, which they didn't five hundred years ago.'

Platters were whisked away and the entertainment began. Tumblers and jesters burst into the hall and evoked cries of admiration at their tricks and acrobatics. The servants sang glees and Christmas songs and the guests were encouraged to join in. Lauren felt she had never had such a happy evening. Impulsively, she reached up and kissed Jake's cheek. He caught her hand and kissed her fingers.

'I'm so glad you've enjoyed it,' he said.

'I don't want it to end. It's been great fun.'

'I think we have to leave this room now,' said Jake as the performers exited the hall. 'Let's go and find some twenty-first century coffee.'

Leaving the Elizabethan rooms behind, they wandered through the candlelit corridors to the tearoom, which had been decorated for a modern Christmas. A huge Christmas tree ablaze with lights and baubles sparkled next to a roaring fire.

Jake chose a table in a quiet corner and ordered coffee. 'I'm glad you've enjoyed this evening,' he said. 'I wasn't sure how Elizabethan minstrels would appeal to you.'

'It's been magical,' Lauren said. 'Thank you so much for bringing me. And I loved the minstrels.'

Jake stirred his coffee thoughtfully. 'Lauren, as we agreed that our friendship was platonic, I must ask — why did you react the way you did when you discovered my sister in my flat?'

She looked away. She had been dreading this question.

'Lauren,' he persisted, 'please answer me.'

'I'm not sure,' she said quietly. 'It was an automatic reaction.'

'Automatic,' he repeated. 'Does that mean that you were rejecting our platonic friendship? That you wanted something else, even subconsciously?'

'I don't think that question is fair,' she answered, lowering her head.

'Because if you *are* rejecting it,' he went on, as if she hadn't spoken, 'I think I'm beginning to feel that way too.'

Lauren's head jerked up. 'You mean ...'

'Yes. I want us to be more than friends. Over the months we've known each other, I've come to realise how I feel about you. Lauren, I think I've fallen in love with you.' His hand reached for hers across the table. 'Tell me that you feel the same way.'

Before she could reply, there was a boisterous 'Ho, ho, ho' from the doorway, and, to general laughter, a larger-than-life Father Christmas strode into the room carrying a sack over his shoulder.

Their romantic interlude disturbed, Lauren and Jake prepared to watch the scene in the middle of the room. Two young girls dressed as elves danced in and began to help Father Christmas distribute the contents of the sack. They gave a little package to each man in the room, while the ladies' gifts were presented by Father Christmas himself.

'This is fun,' said Lauren. 'It's a long time since I had a present from Father Christmas.'

With another 'Ho, ho, ho' from Father Christmas and waves from the dancing elves, the trio left the room to loud applause.

'Can we open our presents?' asked Lauren, looking round at the other people in the room.

'Why not?' Jake was busily opening his. It contained a key ring from which hung a medal bearing a picture of Whittington Court. 'I shall think of this evening every time I look at it.' He wrapped it up and smiled tenderly at Lauren. 'Open yours now.'

Lauren unfastened the pretty Christmas paper and took out a little box. She lifted the lid. Inside was a Christmas decoration of gilded holly leaves and red enamelled berries.

'Oh, isn't it pretty.' She passed it to Jake. 'It'll have a special place on my tree this year.'

A waitress appeared with a coffee pot

and filled their cups again.

'What a lovely evening,' said Lauren happily. 'Did you know it would be like this?'

'No. But I'm glad it's made you happy. Now can you answer my question, or have you forgotten it?'

Lauren blushed. 'I haven't forgotten it. You said that you loved me, and you asked whether I felt the same way.'

'Well?'

She looked straight into his eyes. 'When we first met, we both felt that friendship would be enough. Neither of us was looking for more. Why have you changed your mind?'

He stared at her without speaking for so long that she shook her head. 'Don't look at me like that. People will notice.'

'Let them; I don't care. I'm listing in my mind all the reasons I believe I love you. You're sweet and kind, but also clever. You know what you want from life. You have time for me and Alfi, and also my mother. I couldn't be friends with you any longer and not fall in love with you.'

Lauren smiled at him with tears in her eyes. She picked up her coffee cup, but her hand was shaking and she put it back in the saucer. Jake loved her. It was unbelievable.

He picked up her hand and pressed his lips to her palm. 'Now tell me, could you love me?'

She put a hand over his. 'Yes, I feel the same way. I love you. I have done for some time.'

'How can we sit here just drinking coffee when we've made this wonderful discovery? I love you and you love me.' He laughed. 'We should be drinking champagne, not coffee. And I know one person who'll be very pleased — my sister, Christa. She liked you enormously. She said she was looking forward to getting to know you better.'

'I feel the same about her,' said Lauren. 'I hope I'll see her again soon.'

But there's one person who won't be pleased, Lauren thought. *Jake's mother. She'll never like me.*

As if reading her thoughts, Jake said,

'I'm going down to see my mother on Sunday week. Will you come?'

Lauren's feelings must have shown on her face, because he said hurriedly, 'Please don't say no. I know Mother hasn't been very friendly, but we must make her see that we love each other and that she has to accept it.'

'She'll never accept it. She keeps hoping that you and Marilyn will get together again.'

Jake sat thinking for a few minutes. Then he said, 'I'm going to phone Marilyn tomorrow. She must go and see Mother and make her realise that it's all over between us. Perhaps she should take Rory, her new man, with her.'

'Poor Rory.' Lauren giggled. 'He'll get the same reception as me.'

Jake began to laugh too. 'I don't know why we're laughing. It's a very difficult situation. Marilyn must do her bit. She got herself into Mother's good books; she must get herself out. I refuse to take all the blame for the divorce.'

Lauren reached across the table and

took his hand. 'Why don't you go with Marilyn?' she suggested. 'Perhaps the two of you together could make your mother appreciate the situation.'

'You wouldn't mind?'

'What, you going with Marilyn? Of course not. I'm sure it'd help.'

He put his other hand on top of hers. 'I'll ring her tomorrow. I'm sure she'll agree. Then you and I can go down together later on.' He smiled, pleased that a difficult situation might soon be resolved.

Lauren looked around the room. 'People are beginning to move. Perhaps we should go too.'

'I don't want to leave,' said Jake. 'I have coffee, a Christmas tree, a log fire and you. I want to stay here all night.'

'I don't think the staff would agree,' said Lauren, picking up her bag and coat. 'Come along, we really must go.'

Jake sighed. 'Oh, very well.' He slipped an arm round her waist and they followed the crowd back along the wood-panelled passages to the big front door. They shivered as the cold air struck them.

Lauren looked up at the star-studded sky. 'All we want now are some flakes of snow.'

Jake hurried her towards the car. 'I don't think so. Come along; you don't want to get a chill.'

They climbed in and he switched on the heater. Then he slipped his arm behind her head and pulled her towards him. 'My beautiful, darling Lauren,' he murmured.

Her arm reached across to hold him tightly.

'Tell me again that you love me,' he said.

She pulled away from him and looked into his eyes. 'I love you, Jake, with all my heart.'

He kissed her. 'I forgot another reason for falling in love with you.'

Lauren looked up at him questioningly.

'You're so beautiful,' he murmured against her lips.

10

'Is there any chance you could come down to see Mother with me on Sunday?' Jake asked Marilyn on the telephone the next evening. 'Why? Has anything happened to her?'

'No. But ... well the truth is, I've met someone. Mother has to accept that you and I are going our separate ways.'

'Lauren,' said Marilyn. 'I've heard all about her from your mother.'

'Well you know what I mean,' said Jake. 'I don't suppose she was very kind about Lauren.'

'She said that you introduced her as just a friend.'

'She was. But now we've realised that we want to be more than friends.'

'So why must I come down to Langton Bay?'

Jake sighed. 'Because Mother will listen to you. Because she needs to see us with other partners to know that we'll never get together again.'

There was a silence while Marilyn thought. 'What about Alfi? Would it help if he came?'

'No, I don't think so. Mother would be so preoccupied with him — or pretend to be — that she wouldn't listen to what we say. Could your mother have him overnight?'

'I'm sure she would. All right, I'll come with you. And it's time Rory met her. Why don't the four of us go down together?'

'Thanks, Marilyn. You've put my mind at rest. Come here for coffee on Sunday at ten and then we'll all go together.'

Jake had the largest car, so he had offered to drive on Sunday. The four of them met for coffee first in Jake's flat. The two women eyed each other surreptitiously. At first they were all very quiet, concentrating on the coffee and biscuits. Then Jake broke the silence.

'Thank you all for agreeing to visit my mother,' he said. 'The situation is difficult. She adores Marilyn and cannot accept anyone else in her place, or our divorce. Unless she can be made to see that these things happen, she'll never accept Lauren or Rory, or our new relationships.'

'I've seen her since the divorce,' Marilyn said, 'and it was very sad. She kept breaking into tears and saying that Alfi would suffer without two parents.'

'I've explained to her that Alfi sees me as much as he wants to,' said Jake.

'He and Rory get on so well,' said Marilyn, giving her partner a fond smile. 'He doesn't pretend to be Alfi's father, but they are getting quite close.'

'He's a super kid,' said Rory. 'I'm trying to be ... not a replacement for you —' He nodded to Jake. '— but someone who's there for him when he needs me.'

Lauren sat and watched the other three, feeling that she had nothing to contribute. Alfi seemed to be at the centre of the problem. His parents and Rory, and especially his grandmother, were concerned with his upbringing. She felt herself to be on the outside.

When they finished their coffee, Lauren collected the cups and took them into the kitchen. She listened to the voices from the other room as she ran water into a bowl and began to wash the cups and saucers. How lucky that they were able to discuss their problems in a civilised way without arguments. If only Mrs. Viner could see things as they did.

Marilyn came into the kitchen, found a tea towel and began to dry the dishes. 'Are you and Jake, you know, really serious?' she asked.

'I think so.' Lauren wiped down the draining board and rinsed the cloth. 'It's a new idea. We've only been friends up to now.'

'Don't think I'm interfering, but well, I'd hate to see him get hurt.'

Lauren looked at her. 'Again, you mean?'

'I deserved that. Yes, again. I hurt him, but I'm still fond of him. I'd love him to be happy and cared for again.'

Lauren took the tea towel from the other woman, shook it and draped it over the radiator. 'I can promise you that if I have anything to do with it, he'll be loved and cared for and happy again.'

Marilyn put a hand on Lauren's arm, and they smiled at each other as Jake came into the kitchen.

'Come along, darling,' he said to Lauren. 'We're going now.'

The day was cold but pleasant. There was not much talk in the car. They looked at the countryside as it flashed past and pointed things out to Rory, who had never been that way before.

Soon they were pulling up on Mrs. Viner's drive. Jake gave a deep sigh and applied the handbrake. 'Come along, everyone. I don't suppose Mother will come out to greet us.'

He was right. Mrs. Viner waited until they were all on the porch before opening the door. She gave Jake a kiss and pulled Marilyn into her arms.

'Marilyn! How lovely to see you.' She nodded at Lauren and Rory and led the way into the sitting-room. 'Sit down and make yourselves comfortable.'

It wasn't a room for comfort. Lauren perched on the edge of a hard white leather armchair and wished she was anywhere else.

'Did you book a table at the Lobster Pot, Mother?' asked Jake. 'Remember I said we'd take you out to lunch?'

'Waste of money,' said his mother. 'I've prepared lunch myself. Marilyn can help me serve it, can't you, darling?' She swept Marilyn into the kitchen.

'Can I do anything to help?' asked Lauren.

Mrs. Viner gave her a cold look. 'No thank you, you're a visitor.'

Jake, sitting next to her, looked embarrassed but squeezed her hand. 'After lunch, would you and Rory like to go for a walk while Marilyn and I tackle Mother? It might be awkward for you two.'

'That's a good idea.' Rory seemed relieved. 'What do you think, Lauren?'

'I'm all for it.' She smiled at him. 'If it's too cold to walk around, there are plenty of cafés near the beach.'

* ★ *

Lunch was an awkward affair, but Lauren and Rory had an escape to look forward to.

The meal was delicious. A smoked salmon starter was followed by chicken thighs cooked with tomatoes, peppers and onions. Lauren recognised another of her father's recipes. Mrs. Viner was certainly a fan. But this time she didn't acknowledge that it was a TV recipe. Lauren was glad. She felt she really should reveal that Elvin Tate was her father. She hoped that Mrs. Viner wouldn't resent it if she found out later.

'Your favourite pudding.' Jake's mother beamed at him as she brought in a tray of stumpy glasses containing something pink and white.

'Eton mess.' Jake smiled around at the group. 'I hope everyone loves it as much as I do.'

Their enthusiasm broke the ice, and for a while everyone talked normally about the journey down, television programmes and holidays. But the last topic reintroduced a note of animosity.

'I suppose Alfi will be spending his summer holidays without a mummy and daddy,' said Mrs. Viner.

'He'll get two holidays, one with Marilyn and Rory and one with Lauren and me,' said Jake. 'And of course, if you have him for a week or two, he'll have three holidays.'

Mrs. Viner didn't reply. She stood up. 'Coffee everyone? Come and carry them in for me, Marilyn dear.'

This is the most uncomfortable meal I've ever had, thought Lauren. *Let's get coffee over with and escape.*

But they had to sit for a while longer, drinking coffee and trying desperately to think of topics of conversation that wouldn't cause a prickly comment from the older woman.

At last Jake stood up. 'You're going to show Rory the beach, aren't you?' he said to Lauren. 'It's quite cold. Don't be out too long.'

Mrs. Viner looked startled as they put

on coats and scarves. 'It's far too cold for walking out,' she said, as if feeling that some objection was necessary on her part.

'Do us good,' said Rory cheerfully. 'Walk off that delicious meal.' He put an arm round Lauren's shoulder and hurried her towards the door.

Mrs. Viner was right; it was a bitterly cold day. An icy wind blew off the grey sea, tossing their scarves around and making their eyes water.

Rory tucked Lauren's arm into his and marched her briskly down the hill. 'I can see lights down there,' he said, pointing ahead. 'Life! Possibly cafés.'

In ten minutes they were sitting in a cosy beach café, listening to the hisses and gurgles from a coffee machine and the lively chatter of teenagers, escapees like them from the icy wind.

Rory ordered two drinking chocolates. 'Warm us up faster than coffee.' They removed their scarves, unfastened their coats and sat back, smiling at each other.

'It's a silly thing to say, but isn't this peaceful?' said Lauren.

'I know what you mean. The peace of not having to watch what you say and do.'

'She won't talk to me; she won't let me help. I feel a complete interloper.' Lauren stirred her chocolate and then put down the spoon but didn't pick up the cup. 'I wonder how they're getting on.'

'Don't think about it. Drink your chocolate.' Rory picked up his own cup. 'Let's talk about something else.'

Lauren took a sip. 'How did you and Marilyn meet?'

'We met at school. We were five.'

'Good gracious. So were you childhood sweethearts?'

'Actually, yes. We played together as children and went out as teenagers. Then Marilyn went on holiday and met Jake.'

'But you found each other again on the internet.'

'Marilyn was playing about on one of those friendship sites and reconnected with me. We met up, and the rest, as they say, is history.'

'Poor Jake,' said Lauren instinctively.

'Yes.' Rory looked down at the table. 'I'm sorry about Jake. But if I hadn't taken Marilyn away from him, he wouldn't be free to have you.'

'That's true. I would never have met him.' She finished her drink. 'That was lovely. I'm beginning to feel warm.'

'How did you two meet?'

'Nothing so romantic. He took the flat opposite mine. We just got friendly.'

They grinned at each other. 'So we're all happy,' said Rory. 'There's only Mrs. Viner to convince.'

Lauren looked out of the window. In the dull light of the street lamps she could see the furious waves flinging themselves wildly against the shore. 'I don't think I want to go out into that weather again.'

Rory glanced at the clock over the counter. 'We've been here twenty minutes,' he observed. 'Is that long enough for a peace conference?'

'Let's stay here a bit longer. I really don't want to go back yet.'

'I'll get some more chocolates. We'll drink them, and then we must go back.'

When they returned to the bungalow, they were greeted with a smile from Mrs Viner. Lauren wasn't sure what she expected, but it wasn't a smile. The peace conference, as Rory called it, must have gone well.

'Come and sit by the fire — you must be frozen,' Mrs. Viner insisted. 'We're going to have some tea, then Jake says you must be off.' She bustled into the kitchen while Lauren wondered how she could manage a cup of tea on top of two drinking chocolates.

There was silence in the car for the first few miles as they drove home. 'Well, don't you want to know what happened?' Jake asked at last.

'We didn't want to pry,' said Rory.

'It concerns you two as much as us,' said Marilyn.

'We didn't want to waste time,' said Jake, 'so I told Mother firmly that Marilyn and I were still friends, but settled with new partners. Alfi was well looked after and could spend time with whoever he chose.'

'We said there was no chance whatever of us remarrying.' Marilyn took Rory's hand and smiled up at him.

'I'm afraid we had to be cruel,' sighed Jake. 'I said that if she continued to refuse to acknowledge you two, she would see less of us.'

'And of Alfi,' added Marilyn.

'What did she say?' asked Lauren.

Jake thought for a moment. 'D'you know, she didn't put up any argument at all. I think she had expected it and was resigned.'

'I've promised to take Alfi down to see her next weekend,' said Marilyn. 'That made her happy.'

★　★　★

Lauren decided to accompany her father to the College of Food when he went to present the prizes. She felt it was only fair when he'd agreed to give up his time to please her.

The hall was packed with bright-eyed students, and there was a roar of applause when the principal, Miss Langton, introduced him. 'We are honoured today to have a most distinguished chef and restaurateur to award our prizes,' she said. 'All of you will have seen him on his television programmes, and some lucky people may have eaten at one of his restaurants.'

There were loud whoops from the audience. The students knew the prices at the restaurants were way beyond their purses.

Miss Langton smiled. 'Well I have, and I can tell you it's a most enriching experience. So without any more talking from me ... Mr. Elvin Tate.'

To loud applause, the chef walked to the centre of the stage and took up a position behind a table full of books.

Lauren had taken a seat halfway back in the hall. She didn't want to sit where he could see her and possibly put him off his stride. But she need not have worried. Her father was thoroughly enjoying himself with the young people.

The prizes were cookery books, but the final award of an expensive food mixer was for the student who'd made the most progress in his or her year. Lauren was thrilled to see that Natalie, her work experience student, was the recipient. She clapped until her hands ached.

When the ceremony was over, Margaret escorted her to the principal's room, where drinks and canapés were waiting.

'How lovely that the prize went to Natalie,' said Lauren to Margaret.

'Do you know her?' asked her father.

'She's doing work experience in my shop.'

'Is she.' He looked thoughtful. 'She's very pretty. I wonder if she's photogenic.'

Lauren smiled. She knew what was coming.

'I shall keep an eye on her,' said Elvin Tate. 'She might be just what I want when my present assistant leaves.'

'Why don't you have a plain woman sometimes?' asked Lauren mischievously.

'Because my show is glamorous,' he retorted. 'Glamorous food, glamorous setting, and pretty young assistants to set it all off. When are you coming to join me? You're the prettiest of them all.'

'You wouldn't be biased, would you?' Lauren saw the principal heading towards them and left to find Margaret.

★　★　★

Jason had folded a pile of boxes for the biscuits, so when Lauren arrived at the shop the next morning she was able to start packing. As soon as Colin and Natalie arrived, they took over the job. Lauren looked admiringly at the growing stack of white and gold boxes.

'I'll go and arrange some in the window,' she said.

'Lauren, have you thought of other outlets for them?' Jason queried.

'Other outlets?'

'Yes. What about the food hall at Harrington's? And that specialist grocers in the high street. Why don't you go and see them?'

'That might be a good idea. I'd only thought of selling them here, but if we can cope with demand, it could be profitable.'

Paulina was already hard at work at her special table, decorating rows of biscuits. Lauren stood behind her and watched. 'Angels today,' she commented as the Polish girl added tiny gold halos to each angel. 'You're so clever, Paulina. I'm sure they'll be irresistible. As soon as the shops open, I'll do some phoning; hopefully get some appointments.'

Lauren was reaching out to pick up the telephone when it rang. She was surprised to hear her father's voice.

'What are you doing for dinner tonight, Pidge?' he asked.

'Er, nothing. I haven't thought about dinner.'

'Right. You're coming with me.'

'What do you mean, coming with you? D'you mean dinner at your place?'

'Come here, but we're going somewhere else. Eight o'clock suit you?' He rang off without waiting for her reply.

Lauren sighed. Where did he get his energy? Still, it would save her cooking a meal.

She picked up the telephone again, dialled Harrington's, the town's department store, and asked for the food department.

Half an hour later, she had three appointments to display her biscuits to likely shops. The first one was that afternoon. *Mustn't waste any more time*, she told herself. Christmas was only a month away. She should have contacted customers some time ago, but they might be glad of something new to boost sales at this late date. If not, the contacts would be useful for next year.

* * *

The buyer at Harrington's was captivated with Paulina's designs. 'I've never seen such original biscuits,' she enthused. 'I'm sure we can sell as many as you can let us have.'

Lauren had a moment of doubt. Could they make enough in the time? She'd have to set the students to doing it. It wasn't difficult, and working under pressure would show them what life in a real

201

kitchen was like.

She returned to the shop full of enthusiasm. Jason was pleased that his idea had been fruitful, and Paulina wasn't a bit fazed by a prospective increase in production.

'I can do,' she said confidently. 'No problems.'

The students were happy to make some money by working on a Saturday, so Jason and Lauren felt the new venture had every chance of success.

* * *

Lauren's father was waiting for her when she arrived at La Belle Étoile. 'Where are we going?' she asked.

'La Belle Fleur. Come along. I told them we'd arrive at eight fifteen.'

'La Belle Fleur? Why are we going there? Why don't we eat here?'

Her father opened the door of his car and she slid into the passenger seat. 'Don't ask so many questions. Be grateful for an exquisite meal prepared by Petros.'

Lauren was silent for the rest of the journey. When her father was in one of his odd moods, it was best to wait until he explained himself.

La Belle Fleur was decorated in green and gold like all of Elvin Tate's restaurants, but the emphasis was on flowers to reflect the name. In the centre of the room, a tall floor vase held enormous artificial gold sunflowers. Elvin and Lauren were led to a table next to the flowers.

Petros, the chef, came hurrying out of the kitchen to welcome them. 'My friends, how wonderful to see you,' he greeted them effusively. 'You are just in time. I have prepared for you a beautiful meal.' He kissed the tip of his fingers. 'Just you wait and see.'

Lauren felt Petros overdid his greetings, but her father looked pleased. They handed their coats to a waiter who glided silently up as if on wheels, and settled themselves for the beautiful meal.

They started with Prawns Mariette, crisp pastry tartlets filled with prawns in a cream sauce with just a hint of mustard.

Elvin Tate nodded his approval.

Petros himself brought medallions of beef to their table. He placed the dish in the centre with a flourish and beckoned the waiters to serve tiny carrots and sprouts.

'This *jus* is delicious,' Lauren enthused as she speared a sprout and dipped it in the sauce.

'Red wine and mushrooms and something else, I think,' said her father thoughtfully.

'You're going to miss Petros,' said Lauren.

Her father sighed and laid down his knife and fork. 'Do you like this restaurant?' he asked.

Lauren looked surprised. 'Of course I do. I like them all, but this one is especially glamorous. I suppose it's the flower theme.'

'Well ...'

'Oh no!' Light dawned for Lauren. 'You've brought me here to try and persuade me. I've given you my answer.'

'But you're a trained chef. You came

out top in your year. You've spent time in some of the best kitchens in Paris and Switzerland. How can you be satisfied with —' He spat out the word. '— cakes?'

Lauren was silent. Perhaps her father was right. Perhaps she was wasting her expensive training and all the experiences she'd had abroad. 'You'd still need to get another good chef,' she said.

Elvin Tate sensed she was weakening. 'Of course, and you could help to choose him. I have a shortlist, some excellent candidates.' He put a hand over hers where it lay on the table. 'You'll do it?'

'Come on, don't rush me,' said Lauren. 'If it wasn't that Daisy has left, I wouldn't even consider it. And I might *not* consider it,' she warned him. 'Just leave the idea with me.'

A waiter appeared with a tray and set dishes down before them. 'What have we here?' asked Elvin.

'Chef's special. Lemon cream with fresh raspberries,' said the man.

'How does Petros get fresh raspberries at this time of year?' asked Lauren when the waiter had gone.

'He has secret sources,' her father replied. 'He won't tell even me where he gets some of his ingredients. But it's why people come for miles to eat here.'

'So what will you do when he goes?'

'Find another chef with secret sources, I suppose,' said Elvin with a rueful smile. 'Have you any?'

'You don't need them with cakes,' said Lauren, laying down her spoon. 'That was a wonderful meal. We'll just have some coffee and say goodbye to Petros, then I really must go. I have to make a hundred biscuits before bedtime.'

Elvin Tate shook his head. 'Biscuits,' he said. 'Biscuits and cakes!'

★　★　★

The telephone was ringing as Lauren entered her flat. 'Where have you been?' asked a familiar voice. 'I've been ringing all evening.'

'Daisy! Daisy, how wonderful to hear you. How are you?'

'I've got some wonderful news.' Daisy sounded excited enough to explode. 'You'll never guess.'

'Tell me,'

'I'm going to have a baby. I've had it confirmed today. Morice is so excited. He wants a boy to join him in the band, but I think it'll be a girl.'

'Daisy, I'm so thrilled!' Lauren broke into the flood of excited chatter. 'Can I be a godmother?'

'Better than that. I'm going to name her after you. Baby Lauren.'

'But what if it's a boy?'

'Then it'll be Laurence.'

'Oh Daisy.' Lauren's eyes filled with tears.

'I want to hear how you're getting on with the shop, but I'm too excited to talk about anything except the baby. I'll ring you again in a day or two.'

Lauren put down the phone and stood for a moment lost in thought. A baby. Well, Daisy wouldn't be interested in cakes now. She had much more important things to fill her mind.

Baby Lauren. She smiled to herself. She couldn't wait to tell Jake.

11

Was that Jake? Yes it was, coming out of Maples bookshop. But Jake was no reader. What was he doing in a bookshop?

Lauren waved wildly but couldn't attract his attention. She tried to cross the road but the traffic was unceasing. When she finally found a gap and darted across, Jake had disappeared.

The car park they used was just a few yards down from the bookshop. By now he would have reached his car and probably left by the far entrance.

Disappointed, Lauren gazed unseeing into the window full of bright book covers. Then she noticed a sign in the middle of the window:

COME AND TRY OUR NEW CAFÉ

New café? In a bookshop? What a good idea. Books and coffee went together. Lauren pushed open the door and went in.

She had half an hour or so before she was expected back at the shop. She'd been to Harrington's with their first delivery of biscuits, deciding to take them herself so that she could be sure they had a prime position.

The café was at the back of the shop, a dozen tables in an inviting little annexe. Lauren looked around for a table, then spotted someone she really didn't want to see.

'Come and sit here,' said Pamela. 'It's rather crowded this morning; you won't get a table to yourself.'

Lauren hesitated. She didn't want to sit with Pamela, but it was true, there were no empty tables.

'Please,' wheedled the other woman. 'Can't we be friends? What happened at the dance was an accident. I said I was sorry.'

It wasn't an accident, thought Lauren. *You soaked me deliberately*.

Pamela was pulling out a chair and beckoning to the waitress. 'My treat,' she said. 'What are you having?'

Reluctantly, Lauren sat down.

'How are you?' asked Pamela with false sweetness. 'Jake was looking very well when I saw him last.'

'When was that?' Lauren was immediately suspicious.

'Oh, not long ago.' Pamela studied her nails. 'Of course, I see him regularly at work. I've been promoted, you know. I'm secretary to Jake's immediate boss.'

Not long ago? Like ten minutes? Was that why Jake was in Maples? Had he arranged to meet Pamela?

Before the waitress could bring her coffee, Lauren pushed back her chair and stood up. 'I'm sorry, I can't stay,' she said. 'Goodbye.' She turned and fled through the shop and into the street.

She hurried hack to the shop, biting her lip. Was Pamela just trying to cause trouble, or was she still seeing Jake? It was no use; she'd have to confront him this evening before their relationship went any further.

★ ★ ★

211

Jason looked up from the counter where he was arranging a tray of cream cakes. 'What's up? You look mad.'

'Oh nothing.' Lauren shrugged off her coat. 'I've just met someone I'd hoped never to see again and it upset me.'

'Man or woman?'

'Woman. A very nasty, spiteful ...' She sighed. *I must take a grip on myself. Pamela isn't important enough to upset me like this.* 'Is there any coffee? I was going to stop for one but I changed my mind.'

'Coffee coming up.' Jason went into the kitchen, and Lauren could hear the hiss of the coffee machine as she hung up her coat.

'How did Harrington's like the biscuits?' asked Paulina.

'They absolutely loved them. They've given them a prime position on one side as you go into the department. You can't miss them. They have high hopes of excellent sales.' She sat back in her chair. 'This is good coffee, Jason. I'm glad I didn't stop for one when I was out.'

'What have you planned for tomorrow?' he asked.

'I want to make a lot of the new mince pies. The students can help me. They need to practise their pastry-making. And we'll make some green cupcakes with red berries on top, and those little snowman cakes we tried out last week.'

'Christmas is coming,' sang Jason as he finished his coffee. 'Right, let's start the preparation. Paulina will have to stay with the biscuits, and we'll have to serve in the shop as we work. Thank goodness the students are in again tomorrow.'

'They're a great help, aren't they. I'm glad we decided to take them on.'

★ ★ ★

Lauren left the front door open that evening when she got home from work so that she could see Jake as soon as he reached his door. He noticed the open door and came across.

'Were you waiting for me or someone else?'

She came up to him slowly. Now the moment of confrontation had arrived, it was difficult to know where to begin. 'Jake, I want to ask you something.'

He bent and kissed her on the lips. She pulled back a little. This was difficult enough without the complication of kisses.

He put his arms around her. 'Well what do you want to ask me?'

'I don't know quite how to put this, but I must know, so I'll have to come straight out with it.'

'I'm intrigued. What d'you want to know?'

Lauren gazed up into his face. He looked totally innocent. What was she risking if she asked about Pamela? But she had to know. 'Jake, are you still seeing Pamela?' The question came out baldly.

Jake sat down on the arm of the nearest chair as if from shock. 'Pamela? You mean Pamela at work? Good heavens, no. Whatever made you think that?'

Lauren swallowed. 'I saw you come out of Maples bookshop this morning. It seemed an unlikely place for you to be.'

'I may not read much fiction, but I do occasionally buy books,' he said. 'Why didn't you come and speak to me?'

'I was on the other side of the road. By the time I'd got through the traffic, you'd disappeared.'

'So what has all this to do with Pamela?'

'Maples also has a café.'

'Good for them. I still don't get the point.'

'When you'd gone, I decided to have a coffee before going back to the shop. I went into the café. Pamela was there.'

'So you thought I'd been in there with her.'

'She ... she implied that she'd seen you recently.'

'By recently, you thought she meant a few minutes earlier. That I'd met her there.'

Lauren said nothing.

'I see her at work when I go into the office. She's been made private secretary to Nick, my boss. I don't need to make secret assignations with her.' His voice was quiet but he sounded angry.

'I'm sorry.' Her voice was a whisper. 'I love you.'

'You love me but you don't trust me.'

The telephone in Jake's flat began to ring. With a muttered 'Excuse me,' he hurriedly left the room.

Lauren remained where she was. Jake had left the door open so she was sure he'd come back. She waited.

A few minutes later, he rushed into the room. 'We'll have to continue this discussion another time. That was Marilyn. She's at the Childrens' Hospital. Alfi's had an accident. I must go.'

'Let me come with you.' Lauren picked up her coat.

'No. I'll see you later.' He dashed from the room.

Lauren put a hand to her cheek. He hadn't stopped to kiss her goodbye. And he didn't want her to go with him.

Suddenly the room felt very cold. She switched on the fire and sat close, her arms hugging her shoulders. What should she do now? She should be with him, but he didn't want her.

I don't care what he said; I'm going to the hospital. I want to know what's happened to Alfi. He's important; an argument isn't. She switched off the fire and grabbed her coat.

★ ★ ★

The Childrens' Hospital was only fifteen minutes away. Lauren parked the car and went through the heavy doors into the brightly lit entrance hall with its coloured furniture and cartoon characters on the walls. She went up to the reception desk.

'Alfi Viner — he came in this afternoon, I believe.'

'Are you a relation?' The receptionist was efficient.

'Er, no that is, his father is my fiancé.' That was a slight exaggeration, but it got her a helpful reply. The receptionist put on her glasses and consulted a list. 'I just wanted to speak to him and find out how he is,' Lauren added.

'Alfi Viner, Ward 7. Down that corridor and turn right.'

The corridor seemed endless. Lauren plodded doggedly on, wondering what her reception would be when she eventually found Jake.

I want to be with him, she thought, *whatever he says. And I want to know what happened to poor little Alfi.*

At last she reached the end and turned the corner. It led straight into the waiting room, which was empty except for two people. Jake was sitting with Marilyn clasped in his arms, his right hand stroking her shoulder. Her face was blotched and tear-streaked.

They hadn't seen Lauren, and she jerked back out of sight. She felt a sensation of fear. Had something dreadful happened to Alfi? And might it bring Jake and Marilyn together again? Had she lost him already?

She risked another peep. Marilyn was still held in a firm embrace. What should she do? She could hardly walk in on them as if it was quite natural to see the other woman in Jake's arms. Should she go home? But she must know what had happened to Alfi.

Before she could make a move, she felt her shoulders held by two strong hands. 'What are you doing here?' murmured a soft voice against her ear. 'Are you going in?'

She spun round. 'Rory! I'm so glad to see you. I was wondering what to do. I wanted to find out how Alfi's doing, but I didn't want to intrude.' She gestured towards the waiting room.

Rory assessed the situation with one glance. 'Come on.' With an arm round her shoulders, he led her towards the others.

'Rory! Oh thank goodness you're here.' Marilyn released herself from Jake and threw herself into the other man's arms.

Jake stood up and looked at Lauren. 'So you came,' he said.

'I had to be with you,' she said simply. 'How is Alfi? I couldn't wait to find out until you came home.'

They all sat down on the hard leather chairs. The smell of disinfectant was overpowering. 'He came off his bicycle and hit his head on the kerb,' Jake explained. 'He's in X-ray now but they think he'll be all right.'

As he spoke, a doctor emerged from a room nearby. 'Mr. and Mrs. Viner,' he said, looking at the group. 'Alfi's going to be fine, but we'll keep him in overnight, just to keep an eye on him.'

'Can we see him?' asked Marilyn.

'Just the parents, and one at a time,' replied the doctor. 'We don't want to get him overexcited.'

He led Marilyn down the corridor and out of sight. Lauren, Jake and Rory looked at each other and breathed relieved sighs.

'I can take tomorrow off work and bring Marilyn to collect him, if you like,' Rory said, looking at Jake. 'Or did you want to …?'

Jake looked relieved. 'That would be a big help. I've got an important meeting with a new client tomorrow. Lauren and I will come over to see him in the evening.'

In his turn, Jake paid his short visit to his son. He came back smiling. 'He's very pale but he'll be O.K.'

They left the hospital together. Lauren, watching Marilyn walking with Rory's arm around her, realised how silly she'd been. Jake and Marilyn were Alfi's parents. Of course they would hold each other for comfort when their son was hurt. Subdued by the thought of her earlier reaction, she put her arm through Jake's and linked her fingers through his. He smiled down at her.

'What about a meal?' Rory suggested. 'There's a good place just down the road. It has a large car park. We'll need it; we all have cars with us.'

'Not me,' said Marilyn. 'I came in the ambulance with Alfi.' She was looking better already. Powder had covered the tear streaks and she'd applied some fresh lipstick.

'Dinner?' suggested Rory again. Marilyn nodded. 'I'm quite hungry,' she admitted. 'I've been here for hours, but I couldn't eat before.'

Rory looked at Lauren. 'I'm hungry too.'

It was a happy group that gathered round a table at the Green Man. Relief had broken down any reserve they might have felt at such an emotional time. They had chosen a table near the rough brick fireplace with its heavy wooden mantlepiece and huge log fire.

'This is an attractive place.' Lauren looked around at the light wood-panelled walls covered with old paintings in distressed frames.

'Yes, I've never seen armchairs covered in tweed and check in a bar,' agreed Marilyn. 'They look very comfy.'

'Never mind the decor, what are we eating?' asked Rory.

They settled on lasagne; all except Jake, who wanted fish and chips.

'Fish and chips.' Marilyn wrinkled her nose.

'I never have fish and chips,' said Jake. 'Too fattening. But tonight I don't care.'

Alfi was in all their minds but they didn't mention him. Lauren wanted to know how he came to fall so badly but hesitated to mention the accident. Time later on to talk abut serious things. For now they had to relax the tension.

Lauren would have liked to have driven home with Jake but she had her own car to drive back. She met up with him in the corridor at the top of the stair. They walked to their flats with their arms around each other.

At her door she hesitated. 'Jake, about this evening and Pamela ...'

He put a finger over her lips. 'It's forgotten, and I don't want to hear that name again.'

She twined her arms around his neck. 'Neither do I,' she whispered.

12

The table gleamed from the buffing and polishing Lauren had given it as soon as she came in from work. A vase of peach-coloured roses and pale lemon carnations was flanked by her silver candlesticks. She added tablemats and napkins and stood back to assess her efforts. Perfect.

Now to continue her preparations for the meal. She sliced an avocado in half, removed the stone and filled the centre with juicy prawns. Carefully she spooned Thousand Island dressing over the prawns and added a few slices of lemon.

She glanced at the clock. He should be here in half an hour. Enough time.

Now for the main course. She sliced mushrooms and a pepper and fried them gently in butter. Then she made a sauce, and added the mushrooms and butter and some cubed turkey. Lowering the gas, she covered the pan.

She'd prepared the Crème Monte Carlo the night before. Two glasses half-full of mandarin orange segments waited in the fridge. She only had to add the broken meringue and cream.

This was a quick and easy meal, she thought with satisfaction, but it would show him she hadn't lost her skill as a chef. 'I only hope it tastes good too,' she muttered.

She flew into her bedroom and slipped into the deep plum-coloured dress her father had bought her last Christmas. She'd had time to freshen her make-up at the shop, so she only had to fasten a necklace of silver leaves around her neck and add a splash of scent to feel satisfied with her appearance.

She carried the avocado through to the dining table. There was a tap at the front door. On time. Good. Nothing would spoil. She opened the door.

'Evening, Pidge. This is a lovely surprise.' Her father came in brushing snow from his shoulders and handed her a box of very expensive chocolates. Her eyes widened as she saw the label.

'Guessed you'd already bought wine and flowers' he said, 'so I thought you might appreciate these.'

She kissed his cheek. 'Snowing?'

'Only a dusting.' He took off his coat and she carried it into the bedroom while he examined the table.

'Very nice. Shall I sit down?'

'Please do. We're all ready.'

There was silence as they ate the avocado starter. Elvin laid down his spoon. 'Delicious. I suppose you could use crab instead of prawns.'

Lauren nodded. 'Mm. But we both love prawns, so I chose them.'

In the kitchen she added cream and sherry to the turkey dish. The rice was waiting in the oven. She put the turkey into a serving dish and carried that and the rice to the table. Her father sniffed appreciatively.

'Smells rich and expensive,' he said with a smile. 'Turkey à la King, I presume.'

'I was hoping to surprise you. I might have known I couldn't do it.'

He laughed. 'Shall I open the wine?'

The Turkey à la King was a great success. Elvin Tate was in good form, making Lauren laugh with stories of the mistakes made by the glamorous assistants on his television show.

'Serves you right for choosing dolly birds instead of real cooks,' she said.

'You're a real cook. This meal proves it. Why don't you come and join me?'

'Don't you ever give up?'

He laid down his knife and fork. 'No, and I never shall. We'd make a good team. The show would be even more popular.'

'You're already in the top ten most popular programmes,' she said. 'Don't be greedy.'

As he opened his mouth to reply, she stood up and collected the plates. 'I've got something to discuss with you,' she said. 'Oh not the TV show, but later will do. Let's have dessert first.'

He enjoyed the Crème Monte Carlo as she knew he would. 'You've given me all my favourites,' he said, sitting back in his chair with an expansive smile. 'Prawns, turkey and mandarin oranges. A wonderful meal, Lauren. I congratulate you.'

'For a top chef, you have very simple tastes' she said. 'You're easy to cater for. Now come and sit by the fire and I'll make some coffee.' Lauren was relieved and pleased by her father's opinion. Elvin Tate didn't waste praise where it wasn't deserved.

The room was cosy, the chairs comfortable. Lauren felt pleased and satisfied with her evening. She looked at her father. He was sitting back relaxed in his armchair.

'I like to see you resting. You don't do it often enough, I'm sure.'

'A good meal, a warm room and my favourite daughter,' he said. 'I feel very satisfied. I could almost go to sleep.'

She smiled at him and handed him a cup of coffee.

'But I shan't,' he said hastily. 'I haven't forgotten you want to discuss something. What is it?'

She took another sip of her coffee before answering. And then, as if making up her mind, she said, 'I want to discuss La Belle Fleur.'

He looked instantly attentive. 'You've got someone in mind?'

She nodded. 'Me.'

Carefully he placed his coffee cup on the little table at his side. 'Do I take it that you're changing your mind about your future?'

She didn't answer. He took it for a yes.

'Might I ask why? You were so definite before. What about your cake business?'

'Things haven't been the same since Daisy left. She and I started the business together. We had great plans for expansion and so on. I feel … I don't know … lonely without her.'

'But you have good assistants.'

'Jason and Paulina. Yes, they're good — in fact, they're excellent. But it's not the same. I don't feel I have someone really close to discuss everyday events with. And Jason is a man. That makes a difference.'

Elvin Tate sighed deeply. 'Well, Pidge, I don't know how to say this, but …'

'I know what you're going to say. Taking on La Belle Fleur would be something to do because I'm not happy at the moment. You're afraid I wouldn't give it my whole attention — or enthusiasm.'

'It's possible. You might regret it before long.'

'You're wrong,' she said vehemently. 'I've thought about it. If I take it on, I'd be as enthusiastic as you.'

'If you take it on. You're not absolutely sure?'

'It would depend on you.'

'And what about your shop?'

She didn't speak for a few moments. Then she said, 'I'll sell it as a going concern. It's doing well even without Daisy's input. I'll be finished with cakes. As you said, I'm wasting a good education as a chef. Those years in Paris and Switzerland — I should use the experience.'

After a few moments Elvin said, 'I have no doubts about your ability to do the job …'

'But you doubt my commitment?'

'Not exactly, but I wonder how much you've thought about it, really thought. You wouldn't have your evenings and weekends free.'

'That wouldn't matter; we'd work out a rota. I don't go out many evenings now. I'm usually making cakes.' She gave a little laugh.

'Well at least you haven't a boyfriend to object.'

Lauren poured some more coffee, feeling slightly guilty. She hadn't mentioned Jake to her father, feeling that he might think of him as another Steve.

'Well, actually …' she began.

'Yes? I hope that Australian hasn't come back.'

Lauren sat down. 'It's not Steve, but someone who's taken the same flat. We were just friends at first, but now …'

'What's his name? What does he do?'

'Jake Viner. He's an architect.

'Mm. And am I going to meet him?'

'You can meet him now if you like. I can go and see if he's in.'

'No. I want to be prepared. And I haven't really got time now. Bring him along for a meal. Ring me.' Elvin finished his coffee and glanced at his watch. 'Let's both give the matter of La Belle Fleur some serious thought. You know there's nothing I'd like better than to have you working with me. But we must be quite sure. We'll get in touch next week.'

* * *

Jake visited after dinner the next evening. He looked like a man bursting with a message. 'Are you in a good mood?' he asked Lauren as he took a seat by the fire.

'I think so. Why?'

'Would you explode if I said a certain name to you, a name we said we wouldn't mention again?'

She looked at him warily. 'Pamela?'

He nodded. 'Pamela. You'll be pleased to know she's getting married. And moving away.'

Lauren's face lit up in a big smile. 'That's good news. Who's the, er, lucky man?'

'Nick Redding.'

'But he's your boss.'

'And hers. She's his secretary. Apparently they've been seeing each other for some time, but nobody knew. They're getting married quite soon and moving to our branch on the Isle of Man.'

'Good gracious. Well that is good news. I was going to make coffee, but I think we'll have some wine to celebrate.'

'You're a wicked lady,' he laughed. 'You're not celebrating her marriage but her disappearance.'

Lauren poured two glasses and lifted one up. 'To Pamela and her future — far away.'

★　★　★

Lauren lay sleepless in bed for several nights after her father's visit, thinking of the pros and cons of taking on La Belle Fleur.

She had expected her father to agree instantly to her proposal. She had made up her mind and didn't want to think of it again. But she knew he was right. It couldn't be a spur-of-the-moment decision. They had to think carefully. She knew she could do the job. She was a good chef and an excellent organiser. But it wouldn't be her business as the cake shop was. She couldn't build it into anything bigger.

But many of the day-to-day problems, suppliers and staff would be taken off her. Elvin Tate kept a tight hold on all aspects of his restaurants. Her job would be cooking, overseeing La Belle Fleur, and keeping the customers happy. She would lose many hours of freedom, but she would insist on a really good deputy, and they would work out rotas together.

She thought of Jake with a guilty feeling. If they wanted to see each other, it might be difficult. But of course he could always come to the restaurant. They would have to discuss it.

She tossed and turned, trying to decide what to do. Did she really want to give up her shop? It had meant so much to her, but without Daisy ...

234

Jason had noticed how preoccupied she'd seemed lately, and one morning he asked Paulina to take over the shop and marched Lauren into the kitchen.

'Now sit there.' He indicated a chair at the table. 'Drink this cup of tea and tell me what's bothering you.'

Lauren considered brushing his concern aside, saying there was nothing wrong. But he was a conscientious employee and had become a good friend. He deserved an answer. She drank half of the tea, then put down her cup. 'I'm trying to decide whether to sell this business and take up my father's offer to manage one of his restaurants,' she said without a preamble.

Jason sat down opposite her. 'Quite a decision.'

'If I sell it as a going concern, the new owners will probably keep you and Paulina on,' she said.

'And they might not,' he answered

'And they might not,' she agreed. 'But you have something else to go to after Christmas, don't you?'

'Actually, that's fallen through. Could I ask what's brought this on?'

'So many things,' she said wearily. 'But mostly the fact that my best friend left and went abroad. We had so many plans for the business, and now ...'

'And Paulina and I can't fill the gap?'

She reached across the table and took his hands. 'You and Paulina have been marvellous. Without you, the business would have gone under long ago. This is no criticism of either of you. It's me. I just seem to have lost my enthusiasm. I can't see myself here in another ten years.'

Jason thought for a moment. 'Could I ask you to do nothing for two weeks? Sleep on it. Don't make any hasty decisions.'

'Oh I shan't make any hasty decisions,' she assured him. 'My father said almost the same thing. We're both going to think about it, then have another discussion.'

Paulina came in with a tray of biscuits.

'You two look very serious. Is anything wrong?'

'Nothing at all.' Jason stood up and gave her shoulders a squeeze. 'What have you got there? A new design?'

'Yes. Do you like it?' She placed the tray on the table and they gathered round. 'I think for children,' she said.

She had designed a Christmas stocking with toys peeping out of the top: a doll, a train, a book. 'Some for boys, some for girls,' Paulina said.

'What a lovely idea,' Lauren enthused. 'We'll include a few in each box. What you can do with food colouring and icing sugar amazes me.'

Paulina smiled delightedly and took the tray back into the storeroom. Jason and Lauren looked at each other. They both had the same thought. What would Paulina do if the shop closed and no one took it over? They thought but said nothing.

★   ★   ★

That evening was the last French class until the New Year. Mlle. Royale had decided they would have a Christmas party. Everyone was to bring something to eat and a tiny wrapped present. Lauren found herself looking forward to the evening. Jake wasn't too sure.

'Come on, let your hair down,' said Lauren. 'It'll be something different.'

The classroom was decorated with bunting, and in the centre was a small Christmas tree.

'Mademoiselle must have been here early to get all this ready,' said Jake as they put their contributions on the decorated table. Lauren had brought a plate of her special mince pies, and Jake carried two large bags of crisps.

They greeted other members of the class and found places at a table. The tables had been arranged haphazardly round the room instead of in rows.

'Makes it feel really end-of-term, doesn't it,' said Jake. 'What fun.' He gave Lauren a wicked grin.

Mlle. Royale entered carrying two

bottles of wine. '*Bonsoir, tout le monde*,' she greeted them. '*Vin.*' She held up the bottles. 'Alcohol-free, I'm afraid. Not very French, but it's all we're allowed here.'

Afterwards, they all agreed the party had been great fun. Mademoiselle encouraged them to speak French but didn't make a fuss if they couldn't manage.

Lauren felt she had done quite well. Her extra efforts to expand her vocabulary had helped. She'd stuck pieces of paper with French words on all around her flat, to Jake's amusement. 'Instead of laughing, why don't you do the same?' she suggested.

'You do take it seriously, don't you,' he teased.

Jake had done as little homework as he could get away with. Lauren suspected he'd been like that at school. But his charm and high spirits had excused him.

'One day we might go to France, and it'd be useful if we could speak at least some French,' she said.

'We?' he queried mischievously. 'You

mean you'll come for a weekend in Paris with me?'

Lauren felt confused. 'I didn't mean together,' she protested, not looking at him.

'Pity,' he replied.

On the way home, they discussed whether to continue for another term. 'I wouldn't mind, but I don't like doing homework,' Jake complained.

'You don't do any,' Lauren said with a laugh.

'Of course I do. I do it with you.'

'But that's all you do. You need to do extra to learn a language.'

'What about some private tuition?' He pulled her close and kissed the end of her nose.

'Let's leave decisions about another term until after Christmas,' she said. 'Oh, here's the Old Grey Mare. We don't need a sandwich tonight, do we?'

'No, but we can have a nightcap.'

'Actually, I want to discuss something with you,' she said.

'I don't know why I expect you to

have an opinion one way or the other,' she began when they were settled in the cosy bar, 'but I'd like to discuss it with someone.'

'This sounds mysterious. I'm happy to be a sounding board.'

'I'm thinking of selling the shop.'

He stared at her. 'I need a few more details. Why are you thinking of selling it? What will you do instead?'

For the next hour they talked about La Belle Fleur and her father and the cake shop and Jason and Paulina.

'There's so much to consider,' she said with a sigh. 'Not least that Jason and Paulina would be out of their jobs.'

Jake stared thoughtfully into his glass. 'I suppose that one day you'll own all the restaurants,' he said.

'I hope that won't be for ages.'

'Of course. I just wondered whether it'd be good to make a start with one. Get used to the idea.'

'Mm. You've got a point. But what d'you think of my selling the shop?'

He considered. 'You've worked hard.

It's a credit to you. But you're a trained chef. Would you not get more satisfaction running a successful restaurant?'

She stared into the fire. 'What about Jason and Paulina?'

'Jason will get another position and probably take Paulina with him. It's very considerate of you to think about their futures, but you can't base a decision about your own future on them.'

'No.'

They finished their drinks. 'Another?' Jake offered.

'No, thanks. Let's get back. And thank you for your opinion. In the end I have to make up my own mind.'

He put an arm round her shoulders and gave her a squeeze. 'Take your time. Don't rush into anything.'

13

Lauren hadn't seen Alfi since his accident. Jake gave her regular reports, and the child appeared to have recovered completely.

One evening, Jake produced three theatre tickets for the following Saturday. 'Pantomime,' he said. 'You can come, can't you? Do you like pantomime?'

'I haven't seen one since I was ten,' Lauren admitted. 'I liked them then.'

'So can you come?'

'Yes. Yes, of course.'

'Wonderful. I want you to get to know Alfi better. We'll pick him up on the way. I suppose we should really go to a matinee, but Marilyn's quite happy for him to come in the evening as he can lie in the next morning.'

★ ★ ★

The shop was very busy. They had abandoned the biscuits and concentrated on Christmas cakes and Yule logs. The students had finished their work experience and left for the Christmas holidays.

'I wish we didn't have to go.' Natalie made a face. 'I've so enjoyed it here. Can we come again next term?'

'I think Miss Langton will want us to take two different students,' Lauren said. 'We'll miss you, and you must pop in and see us whenever you're passing.' She was touched to receive a hug from both of them when they left.

'Have you made a decision about taking over the restaurant?' Jason asked one day.

'It's really up to my father now,' she replied. 'I've decided I want to do it, but he hasn't contacted me about it. I don't want to rush him. It's strange — he was keen when I said no, and now that I'm the keen one he's hesitating.'

'I'm sure he feels you both want to be really sure,' said Jason, gathering up some dirty plates and placing them in the dishwasher. Lauren thought he had a strange look on his face.

* * *

On Saturday, Lauren and Jake called at Marilyn's house to collect an excited Alfi.

'I've never seen a pantomime,' he confided to Lauren. 'Mummy's told me about it. It's a story but not the same as television. The people are real.' His eyes widened. 'And the one who's the mother is a man dressed up as a lady.'

Lauren laughed at the expression on his face. 'Are you quite well after your accident?'

'Yes, thank you. But Mummy won't let me ride my bicycle yet.'

'The weather isn't suitable,' Jake said. 'The pavements can be slippery. Wait till summer.'

They had reached the local theatre. Jake parked the car and they walked into the foyer. Alfi looked with pleasure at the extravagantly decorated walls and stairways. 'Wow! Look at that tree!' he exclaimed. A huge Christmas tree decorated with purple and lilac baubles and silver chains dominated one corner.

'Would you like some sweets?' Lauren asked, and then looked quickly at Jake in case she'd made a bad suggestion.

'I think we'll just have an ice cream in the interval,' he said.

They were shown to their seats by a smiling man who told them something of the history of the Edwardian theatre. He teased Alfi, saying that the pantomime was *Sleeping Beauty* when Alfi knew it was *Jack and the Beanstalk*.

'You'd think he'd know what it was if he works here,' Alfi whispered to Jake.

Lauren and Jake exchanged smiles over the child's head. 'Look at the programme,' said Jake. 'It has some puzzles in the back.' While Alfi studied the programme, Jake turned to Lauren.

'Have you been busy today?'

'Very. There's been a run on Christmas cakes. It's too late to make more, but we have quite a few in stock.'

'You have a lady making the large cakes, haven't you?'

'Denise, yes. But she doesn't make all the Christmas cakes. That's Jason's department. She makes Yule logs.'

A spotlight fell on the curtain, illuminating a bright Christmas scene with the words 'Jack and the Beanstalk' in the centre.

'Look,' Alfi squealed. 'Isn't that pretty. Oh, the curtain's going up!'

To spirited music from the band, the curtain rose on a scene of peasants dancing in the village square. With a loud sigh of pleasure, Alfi sat back and prepared to enjoy himself.

★   ★   ★

'Well that went very well,' Jake said as they delivered a tired but happy small boy back to Marilyn's house.

'Thank you so much for taking him,' said Marilyn.

'We had a lovely time,' said Lauren. 'I enjoyed getting to know him a bit more.'

'Well that will be essential for the future.' Marilyn smiled at them both. 'Now I'll get this young man to bed. Will you stay for supper?'

They declined, and as they walked towards the door, Alfi ran after them and took their hands.

'Thank you so much for taking me. It'll be Christmas soon. Wouldn't it be fun if we could all spend it together, me and you and Mummy and Rory?'

The adults looked confused. Jake was the first to recover. 'What a lovely idea,' he said, 'but I'm afraid we've made arrangements for Christmas. Perhaps next year.'

In the car Lauren asked, 'And what are the arrangements for Christmas? Or was that just a get-out?'

Jake looked at his watch. 'It's still early. Let's get some supper and I'll tell you. Do you like Italian food?'

'Love it'

Lauren was silent as they drove to La Giaconda, the town's Italian restaurant. What could Jake have in mind? They'd spend Christmas together, she was sure, but what was the mystery?

'Food first,' said Jake as they settled themselves at a corner table. He looked enquiringly at Lauren over the top of the menu.

'Oh, good old spag bol,' she said. 'It's my favourite. I adore spaghetti carbonara, but it's so fattening.'

'I don't think you need to worry about that.' He looked appraisingly at her slim figure. 'I love carbonara. Let's have that and blow the calories.'

The spaghetti carbonara was delicious, soft, creamy and full of bacon. Lauren laid down her fork with a satisfied sigh. 'Just coffee now, thank you,' she said in answer to the waiter's query. She looked at Jake. 'Christmas?'

'I promised, before I met you, to spend it with my mother. I hope you'll come too.'

'With your mother?' Lauren tried to keep the dismay out of her voice.

'It was her idea — to ask you, I mean.'

'Really?' She found that hard to believe.

'She knew I wouldn't go without you, so she suggested you join us.' Jake looked appealingly at Lauren. 'It wouldn't be just us. Christa will be there with her fiancé, Andy, and an aunt and uncle who are elderly but great fun. And possibly an old friend of Mother's.'

'Quite a crowd,' said Lauren thoughtfully. With so many people, Mrs. Viner wouldn't have too much time for her.

'Your father will be busy at Christmas, won't he?' Jake asked.

'Yes. His restaurants are open all over the holiday. He goes from one to another, enjoying himself and being sociable.'

'And were you going to join him?'

'Possibly. If things had been different, I would have spent the holiday with Daisy and Morice. As it is …' Her voice trailed away.

Jake took her hand and squeezed it. 'Please come.' The simple words, sincerely spoken, went straight to her heart. She gazed at him across the table. How could she spend Christmas without him?

'Of course I'll come.'

He gave her a beaming smile of relief. 'Thank goodness. I was afraid you'd say no. How could I enjoy Christmas without you? I'll find out when Mother is expecting us and we'll make plans.'

'I couldn't leave till Christmas Eve,' she warned him. 'We'll close early if we can, but we expect to be busy that day.

★   ★   ★

Lauren had a pleasant surprise a day or two later. A knock at her door in the early evening revealed a smiling Christa.

'You're coming for Christmas,' she said as she entered the flat, unwinding a huge scarf and flopping into an armchair. 'I'm so pleased. We'll have a lovely holiday.'

'What are you doing here?' asked Lauren. 'I thought you'd go home when you broke up from college.'

'I've been staying with Andy's family for a few days. Now I'm with Jake for two days before I go home. I wondered whether we could have a shopping day tomorrow, Christmas presents and so on.'

'It's early closing at my shop tomorrow. We could have a shopping half-day, if that would do.'

It will have to,' said Christa. 'I'll come to the shop at twelve thirty.'

It was the first shopping trip Lauren had had with another woman since Daisy had left, and she was determined to enjoy it. 'This is a good idea,' she said as they set off. 'I have no clue what to get your mother.'

'Let's go for a quick coffee and make lists,' suggested Christa. 'Perhaps I can give you some ideas.'

Once they were in the café and seated at a table, Lauren said, 'We'll make a list of the people who'll be there for Christmas.' She moved her coffee cup and took a piece of paper and a pen from her bag. 'First, your mother. Chocolates?'

'She loves truffles. And scarves.'

'Scarves?'

'Mm. She has a large collection of silk scarves.'

Lauren wrote 'truffles and scarves', and felt she had made a useful start. 'I know what I'm getting for Jake — a cashmere jumper.'

'Lucky fellow,' said Christa. 'That's another off the list.'

They added the other names, and decided on a book on old London for Andy, who loved to wander around the capital; a flowered umbrella for Audrey, Mother's friend who loves flowers; and bathroom luxuries for Aunt Cynthia.

'Uncle Ben will be a problem,' said Christa. 'We'll have to think as we go along. Jake's pinning a lot of hope on your Christmas visit. He thinks you and Mother will get to like each other over a longer break.' She made a face. 'Mother's difficult, but she's had a hard life. Her parents died when she was small, and she was brought up by a very strict aunt. Then my father left home when Jake and I were children. She had to bring us up on her own while she worked full-time as a teacher. Things have never been easy for her.'

'I suppose Marilyn leaving was another desertion for her.'

'Exactly.' Christa gathered up her bag and gloves. 'Jake hopes you'll fill Marilyn's place.'

Lauren stood up and pushed her chair under the table. *I hope so too*, she thought. *I'll do my best.*

The shops were crowded but packed with gifts, and they found it surprisingly easy to make their choices.

Lauren selected a white silk scarf printed with small black butterflies, and another in soft lilac, for Mrs. Viner. In a specialist chocolate shop she bought a luxurious box of truffles. Christa laughed at the relief on Lauren's face as they left the shop.

'You may well laugh,' Lauren admonished her. 'I've been worrying about what to get your mother since Jake suggested the visit.'

The other presents were straightforward and soon purchased.

'What about this for Uncle Ben?' Christa picked up a game of Solitaire in beautifully polished wood.

'Brilliant!' Lauren paid for it and gave

a sigh of relief. 'All done except for Jake. I know where to get his present.' She led the way to an exclusive-looking men's shop at the end of the town.

'Wow!' Christa exclaimed at the prices on the suits and shirts in the window.

'He's worth it,' said Lauren warmly as they entered the shop and breathed in the smell of expensive leather and after-shave. Lauren went straight to a display of cashmere sweaters and picked up one in soft sage green. 'This one.'

'He'll love that,' said Christa. 'Feel the softness.' She held the sweater to her cheek.

Outside the shop, Lauren stopped with a guilty expression on her face. 'Oh I'm sorry — what about your list? I've been marching you around the shops and you've bought hardly anything.'

'Don't worry,' Christa reassured her. 'I've done most of my shopping already, and I have more free time than you. Come along. Afternoon tea and a gooey cake. We've earned it.'

'It's time you met my father,' said Lauren to Jake the next day. 'We have an invitation for dinner tomorrow night. Can you make it?'

'Of course; I should be delighted. I wondered when we should meet.'

'He can seem rather disapproving,' Lauren warned him. 'I'm his only child and he's rather possessive. He hated Steve.'

'Why?'

'He thought I'd marry Steve and move halfway across the world.'

'What have you told him about us?'

'That we're friends — and maybe something more.'

Jake took her hand and kissed it. 'I've never imagined Elvin Tate to be someone to fear,' he said with a smile. 'He looks so friendly on television.'

'If he takes to you, you'll be fine.'

'And if he doesn't?'

'We'll cross that bridge when we come to it'

* * *

They arrived at La Belle Fleur promptly at eight the next evening. 'Too late would be a cardinal error,' said Lauren. 'Good food mustn't be kept waiting. Rule number one in my father's book.'

Elvin Tate was waiting for them in the foyer. He gave Lauren a kiss and Jake a penetrating stare.

Jake was wearing a charcoal suit and a gleaming white shirt with a flowered tie. Lauren felt proud of him as they walked through the restaurant to her father's table.

'I hope you enjoy your food, young man,' said Elvin.

'I certainly do, sir. I'm really looking forward to this evening.'

'Mm.' The older man beckoned to a waiter nearby. 'I've chosen the meal. I hope you like it.'

Lauren wondered whether her father would go all out to impress Jake, then she realised that he didn't need to try and impress anyone. His reputation went before him. Whatever he served would be impressive.

They started with fresh melon balls flavoured with orange brandy liqueur and went on to escalope of pork in a creamy pepper sauce.

'Delicious,' said Jake as he laid down his knife and fork.

'We'll wait a while before our sweets,' said Elvin, 'then you can choose your own. Let me fill your glasses.'

They sat back in their chairs, and Lauren waited for the questioning which she knew would come.

'You're an architect, Lauren tells me,' Elvin Tate began.

'I'm a junior partner in the firm.'

Elvin looked impressed. 'A large firm?' he enquired.

'Moderately,' Jake replied, 'but we're growing all the time. It's Seldon, Price and Goring.'

'I've heard of them. Very well-known practice. You've done well to be with them.'

Jake smiled and picked up his glass.

'To you and Lauren,' he said, and drank.

While her father asked about the projects Jake was working on at the moment, Lauren watched them both in silence. Jake was calm and relaxed, and Elvin Tate had lost the suspicious look he'd had when they arrived. Lauren smiled to herself. She knew what her father was thinking. If Jake was settled with a well-known firm in this country, he'd hardly want to move abroad.

'Now what would you like?' Elvin asked them. 'Lauren will choose ice cream, I expect.'

'Not this time,' she said. 'Have you any of that Princess Flan I had here once?' She turned to Jake. 'Orange and apricot mousse in a pastry case,' she explained. 'It's gorgeous.'

'I'm afraid I have a sweet tooth,' Jake apologised to Elvin. 'May I have that too?'

Elvin gave an indulgent smile and beckoned to the waiter nearby. 'Have you thought again about La Belle Fleur?' he asked Lauren.

'Yes. I haven't changed my mind. I

want to go for it.'

Elvin Tate pursed his lips. 'Well that's a good thing, because I agree.'

Lauren leaned over and kissed his cheek. 'I've told Jake about it, and he thinks I should go for it too.'

'Does he? You'd have to leave your flat and live at the restaurant. I understand you live in opposite flats.'

The young couple looked at each other. 'We shan't be too far apart,' said Lauren, but she had a horrible feeling that when she vacated her flat, another woman could move in and perhaps take her place in Jake's affections. She looked at him doubtfully.

As if guessing her thoughts, Jake took her hand. 'We shan't be far apart,' he echoed. 'We shall see just as much of each other as we do now, I'll make sure of that.'

'Now I have something to show you.' said Elvin, throwing his napkin onto the table. 'If you're going to run this place, Lauren, you'd better see the living quarters.'

'Living quarters? That sounds a bit austere.' She had memories of some of the cramped accommodation above small restaurants she'd lived in as a child. 'Do I have to live on the premises? I could find somewhere very close nearby.'

Her father opened a door in the side wall of the restaurant and ushered them through. 'Up here.' He led the way up a flight of stairs. 'It'll need cleaning and decorating, as it hasn't been lived in for two years, but I'm sure you can organise that.'

He threw open a door at the top of the stairs and Lauren gasped in surprise. A large room was revealed, almost the size of the restaurant downstairs. At the far end was a wide picture window with views over the countryside beyond the town.

'Oh!' Lauren threw her arms wide. 'What a lovely room. I could really do something with this.' The room was empty, but in her mind she was furnishing it with rich blue carpet and blue flowered curtains and …

She was aware that her father was speaking to her. 'Well, do you want to see the rest of the place?'

He opened more doors: bedroom, kitchen, and bathroom. Lauren wandered from room to room in a daze. She could put her present flat in here several times over.

She turned to her father. 'How long will it take to get it cleaned and decorated?'

'And furnished?' said Jake, who'd been following her around with a puzzled expression on his face. 'I can't understand why your chef didn't want to live here.'

'He has a family — three children. You couldn't have them rampaging around above a restaurant. He has a house opposite, very convenient.' Elvin turned to his daughter. 'I'll get a firm in tomorrow. It won't take long to clean and decorate, and then you can order the furniture. With a bit of luck, you'll be ready for the New Year.'

★ ★ ★

Lauren and Jake were quiet on the journey home, each considering the implications of the evening. For Lauren, there was the exciting prospect of a new job and a new home. Jake thought more soberly that if he wasn't careful, he might lose Lauren.

'Why did your father choose the name La Belle Fleur for that restaurant?' he asked.

'The three restaurants were named for my mother. She chose La Belle Étoile, the beautiful star, herself for their first one. La Belle Anna was named after her. La Belle Fleur, the beautiful flower, because she loved flowers. My father loved her very much. He's never stopped missing her.'

'That's why you're so precious to him.'

They stopped outside her door. 'Don't come in,' she said. 'I feel too tired to talk tonight.'

'And you have a lot to think about,' he said, taking her in his arms. 'Goodnight, my darling. Sweet dreams of your new life.'

'You do think I'm doing the right thing, don't you, Jake?'

'I do. You're wasted running a cake shop, however successful. You need more scope. You've been offered a wonderful opportunity. Take it.' He bent and kissed her gently at first, then fiercely. 'So long as you don't forget me,' he whispered.

★ ★ ★

The next morning, Lauren called Jason into the kitchen. 'I've come to an agreement with my father,' she said. 'I'm going to run La Belle Fleur.'

Jason looked at her. 'And the shop?' he asked.

'I'm afraid I shall have to sell it. It's doing well. There shouldn't be a problem.'

'There isn't a problem. I want to buy it.' Jason had a determined look on his face.

'You?' Lauren sat down in surprise. 'You want to buy it?'

'Paulina and I. We'll run it together.'

'But … but I haven't settled on a selling

price yet.'

'I'm sure you'll be fair,' said Jason. 'Work something out and we'll see if we can make it. But I want to be sure of first refusal.'

'You'll certainly have that,' said Lauren, feeling rather dazed. Jason and Paulina wanted to buy the shop. She certainly hadn't thought of that as a solution to her problem.

★   ★   ★

At eight the next evening, there was a knock at Lauren's door. She looked up from her magazine, puzzled. It couldn't be Jake; he had an evening business meeting and expected to finish late. She went to the door. 'Who is it?'

'Someone you didn't expect to see again,' said a voice. Lauren froze. It couldn't be. But the voice had an Australian accent. She unfastened the door.

14

'Surprise!' Two strong arms picked her up and swung her round. She struggled to free herself.

'Steve! What are you doing here? Where have you come from?'

'Aren't you pleased to see me? Have you missed me?'

'Well … well, I …' Confused, Lauren put her hands to her burning cheeks. Steve was as attractive as ever — tanned, bright-eyed, and full of confidence.

'I'm back,' he said. 'Well, for six months anyway.' He looked towards the door. 'I don't suppose my flat is empty. No, it wouldn't be. Never mind, I can easily find something else. We can take up where we left off.'

Lauren stepped back from him. 'Take up where we left off?' she repeated. 'Don't you think I've moved on? You didn't phone, didn't write. D'you think

I've been sitting here waiting for you to contact me?'

Steve sat down on the arm of the chair behind him. 'O.K., I'm rushing you. It's been a shock seeing me after all this time. But —' He turned a pleading face towards her. '— we had a good time together, didn't we? Can't we start again?'

'No. Things are different now.'

'You mean there's someone else?'

'Yes. And he's not likely to disappear to the other side of the world.'

Steve stood up. 'I see. I'm sorry, Lauren. I shouldn't have come. I'll go.' He gave her one of his cheeky smiles. 'One kiss for old times' sake?'

Lauren was about to refuse when she found herself smiling at the wicked glint in his eye. He'd been important to her once and they'd had some good times together. 'Just one,' she agreed, 'and then you must go.' Steve took her in his arms.

'Just one, and make it a good one,' he murmured. As their lips met, the door behind them opened. Lauren, facing the door, was horrified to see Jake, the welcoming smile fading slowly from his face.

'I'm sorry,' he said tightly, 'I must have the wrong flat.' He closed the door and a few seconds later Lauren heard his door slam.

'What was all that about?' asked Steve.

She pushed him away. 'Please go,' she said. 'Now. At once.'

'Oh, I get it. That's your new man. Shall I explain to him? I'll catch him up. He can't have left the building yet.'

'He hasn't left the building. He has your old flat,' said Lauren automatically. 'Just go. Leave us alone.' Her lip trembling, she was staring in anguish at the door.

Jake had looked so cross. What must he think? Would he believe her explanation? He *had* to believe her. Steve was an old friend; she felt nothing for him now. But why on earth had she agreed to a kiss?

Steve took one look at her and quietly left the room with just the slightest wave of his hand. Lauren subsided onto the nearest chair and put her head in her hands. What should she do? Go and see Jake? Telephone him? Go to bed and let time do its work? She wouldn't sleep with this on her mind.

She stood up and smoothed back her hair. In the mirror she caught sight of her reflection, pale face and large, shadowy eyes. Nothing to attract a man there. Should she put on some lipstick for colour? No. It would look calculating. Quietly, she opened her door and peeped out. No one in the corridor. She crossed to Jake's door and knocked gently.

'Yes?' A reply but not a friendly one.

'Jake, it's me. We must talk.'

'I don't think so. I'm going to bed. I'll see you tomorrow — possibly.'

'Jake.' She had to speak quietly but tried to show her desperation. 'Jake, please come to the door.'

There was a long silence then the door opened a few inches.

'Please let me come in and explain.'

'There's nothing to explain. What I saw was plain enough.'

'We can't talk here. Please let me come in.'

'I'm sorry, Lauren. As I said, I'm going to bed. Go back to your friend. I'll see you tomorrow.'

'He's gone,' Lauren said desperately. 'He's an old friend. He only called in for a few minutes. Jake!' But the door was closed, quietly but firmly.

Lauren sat in an armchair until the early hours going over and over the events of the evening. Jake was being unfair in not letting her explain. He'd accused her of saying she loved him and not trusting him; did he trust her?

She loved him and he'd said he loved her. All her dreams had been coming true. And now …

Why oh why hadn't she thrown Steve out as soon as he began to say silly things? Why had she agreed to a kiss? She hated Steve, but she hated herself more.

*　*　*

Jake had spent as bad a night as Lauren. He too had tossed and turned until the small hours. How could he have been so mistaken in Lauren? One thing he'd instinctively felt since he first met her was that she was honest and truthful.

Truthful! She'd said she loved him. So how could he have opened her door and found her in the arms of another man?

Should he have let her explain last night? But no, he didn't want to listen to lies or excuses. He had the evidence of his own eyes. She was in the arms of another man and kissing him passionately — or, to be fair, was being kissed passionately.

'I'm fed up with this,' he muttered to himself. What time is it?' He reached for his bedroom clock. Six o'clock. He'd get up and have some hot coffee. Might as well give up on sleep.

As he busied himself in the kitchen, his thoughts ranged to and fro. When Marilyn had walked out on what he had imagined was a happy marriage, he'd decided never to get involved with anyone again. You can't trust women, was his belief. Then he'd met Lauren and his ideas had changed. What a fool he'd been. She was no different from all the others.

271

He picked up his coffee mug and took it into the bathroom. A really hot shower would be soothing.

An hour later, dressed in comfortable casual clothes, he went into the kitchen to make some toast. There was no need to hurry. He was working from home for a day or two.

He poured another cup of coffee and reached for the milk. The bottle was empty. Of course; he'd just used it up. He'd left enough last night for this morning's coffee, but he'd had two cups. It would have to be black, which he disliked, unless the milkman ...

Opening the front door, he forgot the milk at the strange sight which met his eyes. Across the corridor, outside Lauren's door, a figure sat on the floor, obviously fast asleep, with a large bouquet of flowers at his side.

Jake stared. The figure must have sensed Jake's presence, because his eyes flickered open.

'Morning,' he said.

'Er ... Good morning,' Jake said. 'Are

272

you waiting for Lauren?'

The young man yawned. 'Yes. I must have dropped off.' They stared at each other. 'You must be the new guy,' said the figure on the floor.

'New guy?'

'Yes. Lauren's new guy. She said you had my old flat.'

So this was the man who was kissing Lauren last night. Jake thought he should really punch him on the nose, but it was a bit early for fisticuffs.

The milkman had been. Jake bent and picked up the bottle. 'Coffee?' he invited.

The man sprang to his feet. 'Now that's really civil of you. I'd love some.' He picked up the flowers and followed Jake into the flat. He looked around admiringly. 'Say, you've made this real cosy.' He placed the flowers on the table. 'Peace offering for Lauren,' he said, 'though I don't suppose she'll ever forgive me.'

'You must be Steve,' said Jake.

'Yeah. Returned like a bad penny. Thought we could take off where we left off. Lauren had other ideas.'

'You mean your return was a surprise to Lauren?'

'Surprise? Shock, more like it. She went mad.'

Jake poured out two mugs of coffee and handed one to Steve. 'Oh, by the way, I'm Jake.' They shook hands.

'Are you and Lauren …?' Steve looked at the other man over the rim of his mug.

'We started as friends when I moved in here. Then we became close. I've loved her for some time and she said she loved me. Now I don't know.'

'You mean … I've spoiled things?'

'I don't know what to think.'

Steve finished his coffee and placed his mug on the table. 'Lauren's a lovely lady. When I was living here we had a thing going. We were both pretty keen. But I'd left a woman back in Oz and I had to go home and see how we felt about each other.' He gave a short laugh. 'She didn't feel anything for me — in fact, she'd got engaged. So when the chance came to come back to the U.K. for six months, I jumped at it. Thought I'd see if Lauren wanted me back.'

'Last night it looked as if she did,' said Jake coldly.

'Don't get things wrong,' said Steve. 'The kiss was my idea. A goodbye kiss. She'd made it quite clear that we were finished and that there was someone else.'

Jake felt for the chair behind him and sat down. I've been a fool,' he said quietly. 'I said I loved her, and I wouldn't even listen when she wanted to explain. I don't deserve her.'

'Don't blame yourself. It must have looked bad,' said Steve. 'And it was all my fault. But it's not too late. Go and see her now. Take these flowers if you like.'

'That's very generous of you,' said Jake. 'But they're your flowers. She'll appreciate them coming from you.'

'I'll leave them outside her door,' said Steve. 'I don't think I'll speak to her.' He held out his hand. 'Goodbye and good luck. I might see you around.'

Ten minutes later, Jake heard Lauren's door open. He stood up, then sat down again. He'd see her tonight.

That evening, Lauren rescued Steve's flowers from the sink where she'd left them that morning. She collected two vases, filled them with water and popped in a small aspirin. Then she started to arrange the blooms, cutting an inch from each stem before she did so.

It was soothing work. She enjoyed arranging flowers. But what a pity they were from Steve. If only Jake had regretted his hasty rebuttal of her last night and bought her some flowers.

When she'd spotted the bouquet in front of her door, she'd imagined they were from Jake. The card soon disillusioned her. 'A peace offering, Lauren. Please forgive me. Steve.'

She finished her flower arranging and carried the vases into the sitting room. They looked beautiful, the golds and oranges echoing the colours of her suite.

It wasn't Steve's fault she had moved on and found someone else. He was only being friendly. She should feel flattered that he'd remembered her and wanted her again.

Feeling slightly more cheerful, she went into the kitchen and surveyed the contents of her fridge. Not very inspiring. She needed a trip to the supermarket, but that would have to wait until tomorrow. She was too tired now.

She lifted a loaf, cheese and butter on to the work surface. Cheese on toast would have to do. She had just switched on the grill and popped a slice of bread underneath when the doorbell rang. Jake! It had to be Jake. Slowly she went to the door.

It *was* Jake. A Jake looking very contrite. 'May I come in?'

She stood aside. He entered and she closed the door. Then in a second, they were in each other's arms.

'My darling, I'm so sorry,' he murmured, nuzzling his face into her neck. 'Please forgive me.'

She pulled herself away and looked at him. 'You mean you forgive me? Why? Oh.' She looked at the flowers. 'You've spoken to Steve.'

'He seems a nice guy,' said Jake. 'We

had coffee together at seven o'clock this morning.'

'You did what?' Lauren began to laugh. 'Coffee at seven o'clock?'

'He was sleeping outside your door with the flowers. He'd been there all night.'

'He's crazy,' said Lauren. 'That's just the sort of thing he'd do.'

Jake joined in the laughter. Then he took her in his arms again. 'Darling Lauren, I'll never doubt you again, I promise.'

In the middle of a very satisfying kiss, they became aware of a smell of burning.

'The toast!' squeaked Lauren. 'Oh my goodness.' She tore herself from his arms and flew into the kitchen. The toast was black and the room full of acrid smoke. Coughing, Jake opened the window.

'That's my supper gone up in smoke,' said Lauren ruefully.

'How would you like a chicken casserole?'

'I'd love it, but I haven't got one.'

'But I have, and there's enough for two.

I made it this morning. I've been working at home today.'

'I didn't know you could cook things like chicken casserole.'

'There's a lot we don't know about each other,' he said. 'It'll be fun finding out. Come along. Your supper awaits.'

15

Lauren had so much on her mind in the last few days before Christmas that she wondered why her head didn't explode. But somehow, solving each problem spurred her on to deal with the next one.

Now that they had made up their minds to buy her cake business, Jason and Paulina worked with even more enthusiasm than before. 'We're going to continue with the biscuits,' Jason told her. 'Paulina has some new ideas — biscuits with an Easter theme, a Valentine's one, Bonfire Night with fireworks, and so on.'

'And we will have more students,' Paulina said. 'They are most helpful.'

'Denise will continue to make the large cakes,' said Jason. 'We spoke to her yesterday.'

'And the extra kitchen? That'll be expensive. Will you do it?'

'I have some quotations. I think we can

manage it.'

Lauren looked at their happy faces. To think she'd been concerned about their futures.

'My uncle and aunt in Cracow have helped us,' Paulina confided. 'They have no children, and their café was to be mine when they … you know. But they have sold it and sent me some money to help with the cost of this shop. I'm so lucky.' She flung her arms around Lauren and hugged her.

Lauren smiled at the beautiful Polish woman.'Your English is so good now. You learn so quickly.'

'It is Jason.' Paulina smiled. 'He has teached — has taught me so many things.' She blushed and smiled at Jason, who crossed the kitchen and put his arms around her.

'Shall we tell her now?' he asked her. Paulina nodded. 'In the New Year, when we're properly settled in the shop, we're going to be married,' he said to Lauren.

'Oh, I'm so happy for you.' Lauren hugged them both. 'What a wonderful start to a New Year.'

'And you're making a new start too,' said Jason. 'In your restaurant.'

'You must have your wedding reception there,' said Lauren. 'It'll be my present to you.'

★ ★ ★

There was much to be done concerning Lauren's takeover of La Belle Fleur, but her father had suggested that all should be left until after Christmas.

Lauren couldn't help beginning to think of her redecoration of the flat. She had collected magazines which featured interior decorating and sheaves of paint charts and curtain samples. She read these in bed and fell asleep dreaming of carpets and curtains.

'When are you leaving the flat?' Jake asked one evening. 'You haven't started to pack yet.'

'You sound in a hurry to see me go,' she teased. 'Are you looking forward to having a new neighbour?'

They were cuddled up on her small couch in front of the fire, half-heartedly watching a film.

'D'you want to see the end of this?' she asked and switched off the television when he shook his head. 'Jason has insisted that I leave at eleven o'clock on Christmas Eve,' she said, 'to give us time to get to your mother's house. I think he and Paulina want to close the shop and pretend it's already their business.'

'Do you want me to pick you up from the shop?'

'No, I'll come back here. I'll need to change and collect my presents.' She indicated a pile of brightly coloured parcels under her miniscule Christmas tree in the corner. 'I spent all yesterday evening wrapping them. I hope people will like my choices.'

'I'm sure they will. It's hard choosing gifts for people you don't know.'

'How long has Christa been engaged to Andy?'

'About a year. They're getting married in the summer. He's very nice. I'm sure they'll be happy.' He wrapped his arms round her and held her close. 'That's enough about other people. Have I told you lately how much I love you?'

'I think you mentioned it when you came in. But you can always tell me again.'

★　★　★

Christmas Eve was busy at the shop. Paulina's biscuits were pounced on by people buying last-minute gifts.

'Should we take down the Christmas decorations?' asked Lauren, looking at the tall, narrow tree sparkling with lights and baubles. 'It seems a shame when we're still open.'

'Leave them. We'll come and clear up in the holiday,' said Jason. 'I hate to see decorations taken down before we've even got to Christmas Day.'

Paulina came in with a box. 'One Christmas cake and two boxes of biscuits,' she said, 'and two boxes of your special mince pies. I hope they like them.'

'With Mrs. Viner one never knows,'

said Lauren. 'I expect she's made a cake and won't want mine.'

'I hope you have a happy Christmas.' Paulina took Lauren's hands. You deserve it. You have been so kind to me.'

'Without you and Jason, I don't know how I would have coped.' Lauren squeezed Paulina's hands. 'Happy Christmas to you too. Have a good rest. Next year will be very busy.'

'It's eleven o'clock — time you went,' said Jason. He gave her a hug and a kiss on the cheek. Happy Christmas, Lauren.'

★ ★ ★

Lauren was amazed at the change in the atmosphere in Mrs. Viner's house when they arrived later that day. A large Christmas tree, elegantly decorated with lights and crimson satin bows, welcomed them in the hall. And in the sitting-room, another even bigger tree gleamed with green and blue decorations.

'They must have taken you ages to decorate,' Lauren said to Mrs. Viner.

'They're beautiful.'

Mrs. Viner, who hadn't gone as far as embracing Lauren, nevertheless had greeted her warmly and was delighted with the praise.

'I love Christmas,' she said. 'Nothing is too much trouble at this time of year.'

Christa's fiancé, Andy, a stocky young man as quiet as his fiancée was bubbly, shyly kissed Lauren's cheek and helped her place her gifts under a tree. Christa gave her an exuberant hug.

'I'm so pleased you came,' she whispered. 'It's like having a sister for Christmas.'

Mrs. Viner's friend, Audrey, a retired headmistress, seemed severe and forbidding, but Lauren was sure she could see a twinkle in her eye as they shook hands. Audrey gave Jake a kiss; he was obviously a favourite.

The last members of the group were Auntie Cyn and Uncle Boo. They insisted that everyone call them that. Lauren never did find out their real names. They were both about eighty, but obviously had come to enjoy themselves. The slightest thing set them laughing, and Uncle Boo was full of the most awful jokes.

'Would you like to hear a Christmas joke?' he asked Lauren. 'What did the bald man say when he got a comb for Christmas?' She waited, knowing she couldn't think of the answer. 'Thanks, I'll never part with it.' Uncle Boo roared with laughter and they couldn't help joining in.

'What do monkeys sing at Christmas?' Again they waited. 'Jungle bells, jungle bells,' sang Uncle Boo. Auntie Cyn, who must have heard them all many times before, laughed till the tears ran down her cheeks.

'Thank you, Uncle Boo,' said Jake. 'Let's save the rest till later.'

Their evening meal was a sumptuous buffet laid out in the kitchen. Everyone filled a plate, took it back into the sitting-room, and settled down to watch a comedy programme on the television.

'We don't watch television at Christmas,' said Jake, 'apart from this programme while we eat. We prefer games and charades.'

'Lovely,' said Auntie Cyn. 'A real old-fashioned Christmas.'

'Who wants to go to Midnight Mass,' asked Christa, 'other than Andy and me?'

'I'd like to go.' Lauren looked at Jake and he nodded.

'If you don't mind, I think we'll stay here.' Uncle Boo looked at his wife.

'I agree. I think it's a bit slippery out there. I'm afraid of falling.'

Christa looked at her mother. 'Mum, perhaps you'd better not go if it's frosty.'

'Nonsense,' said Mrs. Viner briskly. 'Audrey and I always go to Midnight Mass. We'll hold each other up.'

They decided to walk to the church, which was only at the end of the road. Aunt Cyn and Uncle Boo waved them off and went back into the warmth of the house.

The little group of churchgoers set off, walking gingerly and holding each other's arms. The road glinted with specks of frost. The church, when they reached it, was bright and cosy and filled with the smell of warm oil radiators.

Midnight Mass was a novelty for Lauren. Her parents had always been too busy in their restaurants to go to church on Christmas Eve. But Lauren knew all the lovely old Christmas carols from her school days and joined in the singing enthusiastically. She smiled at Jake as he sang loudly, barely looking at his hymn book.

'I used to be a choirboy here,' he whispered. 'This is like old times.'

When the service was over, they joined the crowds leaving the church and shouting 'Merry Christmas' to each other. Mrs. Viner and Christa greeted friends while the others shivered in the cold and hoped they wouldn't talk for too long.

At last they all set off for home. They linked arms and walked very slowly and carefully, holding each other up when they started to slip.

'I wish we'd brought the car,' Jake grumbled. 'It'd be better than this.'

'Nearly there.' Mrs. Viner released the arms supporting her to push open the gate. No one knew how it happened, but somehow she lost her balance and fell onto her side on the frozen path.

With difficulty, Jake and Andy got her on to her feet and half-carried her to the house. The fall had given her a shock. She made no fuss but was obviously in pain. Wincing, she lowered herself into an armchair near the fire while the others debated what to do.

'Perhaps we should take her to the hospital, to A&E,' said Christa.

'Oh no,' said her mother. 'I'll be all right. Make some tea and I'll take some painkillers.'

Looking very worried, Christa went into the kitchen. Lauren followed. 'She really should go to the hospital,' she said.

'She's as tough as old boots.' Christa filled the kettle. 'If she says she won't go, she won't go.'

'Well, I don't think she can have broken anything. She went down quite gently.'

'She'll be stiff tomorrow and probably bruised.' Christa collected cups and saucers and put them on the tray. 'What a thing to happen now with a house full of guests.'

'We'll all help,' said Lauren. 'She won't need to wait on us.'

'You know my mother. She likes everything to be perfect. She'd hate the thought of guests looking after themselves.'

They carried the tea into the sitting room. Mrs. Viner had a little more colour but was sitting awkwardly in her armchair. Everyone else sat about looking worried.

Mrs. Viner drank her tea, swallowed two paracetamol and tried to look cheerful. 'I'll be fine by tomorrow. If I can have a good night's sleep, I'll be right as rain. Please don't worry about me. It's Christmas; we should be enjoying ourselves.' She replaced her cup on the tray with a shaking hand. 'Jake, can you help me upstairs, darling? I think I'll be better in bed.'

Jake helped her to her feet, but she collapsed into the chair again with a little cry of pain. 'If I can just get up to my bed

I'll be all right,' she insisted.

'I'll heat some hot water bottles.' Christa disappeared and Jake and Andy managed to get Mrs. Viner to her feet. Progressing very slowly, they helped her upstairs and into her bedroom.

Christa handed the hot water bottles to Lauren to fill while she went upstairs to help her mother undress. She came down looking worried. 'She's dreadfully upset,' she reported. 'She's just remembered Christmas dinner tomorrow. If she can't stand, how can she cook it?' They looked at each other.

'I can help,' said Audrey, 'but I can't be responsible for the meal. I'm a dreadful cook.'

'So am I,' said Christa. 'Mother always did all the cooking and would never let me help. It's a good thing Andy loves cooking, or we'd starve when we're married.'

'I love cooking,' Andy agreed, 'but I've never done a large meal for eight.'

Jake looked at Lauren. 'I hate to suggest it, but ...'

'Of course,' said Lauren. 'Shall we go

and see her?' Followed by the mystified glances of the others, they left the room.

Mrs. Viner was propped up in bed looking very woebegone. 'Oh, Jake.' She held out her arms to him. 'I wanted it to be a lovely Christmas and now I've spoiled it for everyone.'

He hugged her. 'We've got the solution,' he said, beckoning to Lauren, who was hovering in the doorway. 'Lauren will do the meal, and I guarantee you'll be delighted with it.'

'It's very kind of her, but Lauren makes cakes. It's a bit different cooking a Christmas dinner for eight people.'

'Mrs. Viner, I'm a trained chef,' said Lauren. 'Running a cake shop was something I chose to do rather than copy my father.'

Mrs. Viner looked doubtful. 'Your father is a chef?'

Jake gave her a wide grin. 'Your favourite chef,' he said.

'My favourite ... You don't mean ...?'

'Yes. Lauren's father is Elvin Tate.'

'Oh.' His mother covered her face with

her hands. 'I don't know what to say.'

'If Jake can get me some paper and a pen, and you tell me what you've planned for the meal, you can go to sleep and forget about it,' said Lauren. 'I promise you everything will be fine.'

★ ★ ★

Early the next morning, Lauren, with Andy as her willing helper, started on the marathon of cooking what was Christmas dinner. Every so often someone would appear in the doorway to watch the preparations and offer, half-heartedly, to help.

At eleven Mrs. Viner came slowly downstairs, insisting that she felt much better but not stirring from her armchair once she was settled. Christa and Audrey offered to lay the table under her specific directions. Neither was prepared to make any decisions on her own. Mrs. Viner had a theme of dark green and gold, with gold placemats and goblets and green shiny paper holly leaves scattered across the table. Uncle Boo and Jake saw to the drinks, taking as long over it as they could to avoid being given more jobs.

At last, all was ready to Mrs. Viner's satisfaction. Lauren and Andy brought the smoked salmon starters to the table and they all took their places.

Mrs. Viner refused to stay in her arm-chair and use a tray. She took her place at the head of the table and, though obviously in pain, insisted on staying there until the end of the meal.

'You have to admire her spirit,' Lauren said to Andy in the kitchen. 'She won't give in.'

The turkey was cooked to perfection, the roast potatoes crispy, and all the vegetables delicious with just the right accompaniments. Lauren flushed at the compliments showered on her. Jake sat beaming with pride.

Andy made her sit with the others while he served the Christmas pudding. 'I feel as if I've had a cookery lesson today,' he said, to general laughter.

When everyone had finished, Uncle

Boo stood up. 'A vote of thanks to our wonderful chef for a wonderful meal,' he said, and Lauren blushed at the applause.

Mrs. Viner raised a hand. 'Thank you, Lauren, for coming to our rescue. It was a superb Christmas dinner, almost worth having a fall for.'

'But don't think of doing it next year,' said Jake. He stood up. 'A round of applause for the assistant chef.'

Andy blushed as he got applause and a cheer.

'Now,' said Jake, 'let's take our coffee into the sitting-room while we open our presents.'

'Clear up first,' insisted Lauren. Get it out of the way and we can relax.'

There was a general murmur of agreement, and everyone helped. At last the kitchen was returned to its usual immaculate state, coffee was made, and the exciting job of opening presents began.

Lauren's presents were very well received. Jake loved his sweater, and when Mrs. Viner opened one of her gifts and discovered Elvin Tate's latest cookery book with a special personal message to her, she was overcome.

Andy went into the kitchen to make more coffee and came back with a big grin on his face. 'Guess what! It's snowing! We've got a white Christmas.'

They crowded to the window and looked out. Large white flakes swirled and danced in the golden light that spilled out from the house.

'It won't last,' said Uncle Boo.

'We don't want it to last,' said Christa. 'We just want a white Christmas.'

In the excited chatter, Jake drew Lauren into the kitchen. 'Get your coat on, we're going outside.'

'Why? It'll be cold out there.'

'Don't argue. Get your coat.'

They crept into the garden. Snowflakes glistened on Lauren's hair and melted on her nose. She laughed as she brushed them away.

Jake wrapped his arms around her. 'You're not cold now,' he said. 'I'm keeping you warm. I'll always keep you warm and safe.' His lips found hers in an icy kiss.

He slipped down on to one knee. 'My darling Lauren, will you marry me?'

Lauren began to laugh again. 'Get up. Your knee will be soaking.'

'Not until you give me an answer.'

'Yes, of course I will.'

With a sigh of relief, Jake rose to his feet.' My knee *is* soaking.'

'Why did you have to bring me out here to propose?'

'Would you have preferred the kitchen? This is romantic. Just you and me in the snow.'

Lauren flung her arms around him. 'At least life with you shouldn't be boring. Now, can we go in out of the snow? I'm freezing.'

In the kitchen, divested of their wet coats and shoes, and leaning against the radiator, Jake gave a groan. 'Oh no.'

'What's wrong?'

'We'll have to go outside again.'

'No way. What are you talking about?'

'I proposed to you. You said yes. But what did I forget?' He reached into his pocket and brought out a small box.

Lauren held her breath. How could they have forgotten the ring? She opened the box. 'Oh, it's like a sparkling snowflake,' she whispered. A large diamond sat in the middle of a double circle of tiny diamonds, set in platinum. 'It's beautiful.'

She took it carefully from its velvet bed and handed it to Jake, who slipped it onto her finger. It fitted perfectly.

'What a wonderful Christmas,' Lauren said, leaning against him and gazing at her ring.

'Are you two going to spend all of Christmas in the kitchen?' It was Christa in the doorway.

Lauren waved a hand at her so that she could see the ring.

Christa gave a little squeal and rushed to embrace them both. 'A sister for Christmas,' she said. 'The present I wanted.'

There was a chorus of congratulations when they returned to the others. Mrs. Viner beckoned to Lauren, who knelt by her armchair. Jake's mother put her arms around her.

'Welcome to the family,' she said, and kissed Lauren's forehead.

Lauren returned to Jake with tears in her eyes but a happy smile on her face. He pressed a flat gift- wrapped parcel into her hands.

'But you've given me so much already.' Lauren indicated the pile of books, chocolates and toiletries by her chair.

'Open it. See if you approve.'

She removed the paper. Inside was a small watercolour painting of a cottage overlooking the sea. 'It's sweet. Did you do it? I didn't know you could paint.'

'It's for you. Do you approve?'

'Approve?' Lauren turned a puzzled face to him. 'It's a lovely painting. I shall hang it near my bed.'

'But do you like the cottage?'

'I don't understand.'

Jake threw his arms round her and hugged her. 'The cottage is for you. I'm building it on the cliffs about ten miles from here. It's your wedding present. You wanted a house overlooking the sea. We'll be able to spend every summer there.'

'Oh Jake, I can't believe it.' She handed the painting to Christa, who passed it around the group.

'When will you get married?' asked Auntie Cyn. 'Boo and I want to dance at your wedding, but if you wait too long, we might not be capable.' She gave a loud laugh and Uncle Boo joined in.

Later on, looking back, Lauren felt that Christmas afternoon and evening had passed like a dream. They played charades and hunt the thimble. They even danced in a tiny square in the centre of the room. They ate a lovely supper and nibbled chocolates and tangerines. It was the sort of family Christmas Lauren had never known.

At last, when everyone else had gone to bed, Lauren and Jake settled down on the large couch in the firelight.

'This has been a most wonderful Christmas,' Lauren said, nestling happily into Jake's arms. 'I've enjoyed every minute, but I'm enjoying this most of all.' She gazed at her ring.

'When should we get married?' Jake asked, his lips against her hair.

Lauren looked up into his eyes. 'As soon as possible.'

'Shall we say, one month from today? I'd better put it in my new Christmas diary in case I forget.'

'You won't forget. I'll remind you every day.'

'And where should we go for our honeymoon?'

Lauren thought. 'I'd like to go to America and see Daisy,' she said, 'but I think in view of all your hard work this winter, we should go to France.'

'A good idea. Not Paris — too obvious. We'll go to the south. It'll be warmer there.'

Lauren nodded.

'I've done some more French home-work,' he said. *'Je t'aime, ma belle* Lauren.' He kissed her. 'I love you, my beautiful Lauren.

We do hope that you have enjoyed reading this large print book.

Did you know that all of our titles are available for purchase?

We publish a wide range of high quality large print books including:
Romances, Mysteries, Classics
General Fiction
Non Fiction and Westerns

Special interest titles available in large print are:
The Little Oxford Dictionary
Music Book, Song Book
Hymn Book, Service Book

Also available from us courtesy of Oxford University Press:
Young Readers' Dictionary
(large print edition)
Young Readers' Thesaurus
(large print edition)

For further information or a free brochure, please contact us at:
Ulverscroft Large Print Books Ltd.,
The Green, Bradgate Road, Anstey,
Leicester, LE7 7FU, England.
Tel: (00 44) **0116 236 4325**
Fax: (00 44) **0116 234 0205**

AN ORDINARY GIFT

Jan Jones

New job. New town. New house. Everything Clare needs for a fresh start. She could do without the ghosts, though . . . determined to put an unhappy love affair behind her, Clare moves to Ely in the Cambridgeshire Fens to catalogue an early music library. But why does the house she rents in this ancient city feel so familiar? Who is singing Gregorian chants that only she can hear? And what can she do about her growing attraction to Ewan, the site manager of the library, when neither wants a rebound relationship?

AN UNEXPECTED LOVE

Angela Britnell

Kieran O'Neill, a Nashville song-writer, is in Cornwall, sorting through his late Great-Uncle Peter's house. Since being betrayed by Helen, his former girlfriend and cowriter, falling in love has been the last thing on his mind . . . Sandi Thomas, a struggling single mother, has put aside her own artistic dreams — and any chance of a personal life — to concentrate on raising her son, Pip. But as feelings begin to grow between Kieran and Sandi, might they finally become the family they've both been searching for?

PALACE OF DECEPTION

Helena Fairfax

When a Mediterranean princess disappears with just weeks to go before her investiture, Lizzie Smith takes on the acting role of her life — she is to impersonate Princess Charlotte so that the ceremony can go ahead. As Lizzie immerses herself in preparation, her only confidante is Léon, her quiet bodyguard. In the glamorous setting of the Palace of Montverrier, Lizzie begins to fall for Léon. But what secrets is he keeping from her? And who can she really trust?